"I'm re
your willingness to help ⎯⎯⎯

The girl he remembered would have stared at the floor in embarrassment. This new Nola didn't look away, though the tint in her cheeks deepened. "I'm glad. I—I've thought about you often."

He had forgotten the color of her eyes—a pale blue-gray, like shadows on snow. The ash-blond hair he remembered as hanging halfway down her back was now cut in short, tousled wisps that revealed the shape of her head, her small, pearl-pink ears.

"What really brings you back, Nola Shannon? Why are you here?"

She kept her chin up, held his gaze with her own. But she couldn't answer his question.

Because she couldn't remember what she'd come for...or what she'd planned to do when, after twelve long years, she once again stood face-to-face with Mason Reed.

Dear Reader,

We hope you already know that Harlequin American Romance publishes heartwarming stories about the comforts of home and the joys of family. To celebrate our twenty-fifth year, we're pleased to present a special miniseries that sings the praises of the home state of six different authors, and shares the many trials and delights of being a parent.

Welcome to the second book in our THE STATE OF PARENTHOOD miniseries, *Smoky Mountain Reunion*. Have you ever had a crush on a teacher? Well, what if you met that teacher several years later and you still had feelings for him? And what if it turns out he's a single father? Lynnette Kent's book is set in the Smoky Mountains of North Carolina, and I know you're going to enjoy watching romance blossom in this glorious setting.

There are five other books in the series. Last month (June '08) Tina Leonard's *Texas Lullaby* showed us an irresistible bachelor discovering the joys of fatherhood in his instant family. In August *Cowboy Dad* by Cathy McDavid tells the story of an ex-rodeo rider and a woman who knows better than to trust any man who's ever gone eight seconds on a bronc. Watch for more books by authors Tanya Michaels, Margot Early and Laura Marie Altom.

We hope these romantic stories inspire you to celebrate where you live—because any place you raise a child is home.

Wishing you happy reading,

Kathleen Scheibling
Senior Editor
Harlequin American Romance

Smoky Mountain Reunion

LYNNETTE KENT

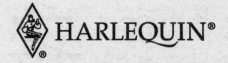

HARLEQUIN®

TORONTO • NEW YORK • LONDON
AMSTERDAM • PARIS • SYDNEY • HAMBURG
STOCKHOLM • ATHENS • TOKYO • MILAN • MADRID
PRAGUE • WARSAW • BUDAPEST • AUCKLAND

ISBN-13: 978-0-373-75221-8
ISBN-10: 0-373-75221-0

SMOKY MOUNTAIN REUNION

ABOUT THE AUTHOR

Lynnette Kent began writing her first romance in the fourth grade, about a ship's stowaway who would fall in love with her captain, Christopher Columbus. Years of scribbling later, her husband suggested she write one of those "Harlequin romances" she loved to read. With his patience and her two daughters' support, Lynnette realized her dream of being a published novelist. She now lives in North Carolina, where she divides her time between books—writing and reading—and the horses she adores. Feel free to contact Lynnette via her Web site, www.lynnette-kent.com, or with a letter to PMB 304, Westwood Shopping Center, Fayetteville, NC 28314.

Books by Lynnette Kent

For Pam, again, because she asks all the right questions and nags until I uncover the answers.

Chapter One

The bad news glared at her from the computer screen.

With her spine stiff and her muscles tight, Nola Shannon stared at the monitor.

She'd dropped by her office at the university to pick up a couple of books, and made the mistake of answering the phone when it rang. Now...

Was she *insane?* What had she just agreed to?

"Nola?" A hand jiggled her shoulder. "Nola? You okay?"

She jerked her head around to look at the man standing next to her. "Oh, Ted. Hi."

He frowned at her, his high forehead wrinkled in concern. "Hi, yourself. I looked in and you were sitting there like you'd been hypnotized."

"I, um..." She pressed her fingertips against her eyelids for a moment, trying to make her brain work. "I had a phone call."

Ted braced a hand on the arm of her chair and leaned in to study the Web page. "Hawkridge? What's that?"

"The Hawkridge School." Nola leaned against the opposite arm of the chair to give herself some space. "That's who called. The headmistress asked me to fill in for a teacher on maternity leave."

Straightening up, Ted propped a hip on the corner of her desk. "Headmistress? What kind of college has a headmistress?"

"Not a college." Nola eased her rolling chair back from the desk. "I'll be teaching math to grades nine through twelve."

"High school? She wants *you* to teach high school?" He shook his head. "That's some nerve, asking an Ivy League Ph.D. to fill in as a substitute teacher."

"I graduated from Hawkridge," Nola explained. "They sometimes approach alumni to help them out in emergencies like this."

"I still don't get it. Most high schools are glad to see the last of their students."

"Hawkridge is…different. Their students have more at stake than just grades and a diploma."

Stepping sideways, Ted settled his six-foot-four frame into a spare chair by Nola's desk. "Explain?"

More than anyone Nola knew, Ted had the right to ask. They'd been friends since graduate school, but over the past few months, their casual evenings together had taken on an aura of romance. He held her hand now, when they went to see a film, put his arm around her as they strolled along the sidewalk. His good-night kisses were lasting longer and longer.

And Nola had recently decided to cooperate. Ted Winfield was a very nice man, a colleague nearly as successful in his field, history, as she was in mathematics. They were both on tenure-track at the university, which would mean employment there for life. Tall and thin, with his blond hair receding slightly but still plentiful, he looked exactly right for the part of a considerate easy-to-live-with husband. Together, they could produce intelligent, easy-to-care-for children.

"Hawkridge is a school for girls with problems," she told him. "Emotional problems that are leading them into dangerous behaviors."

"*You* went there?"

"Yes." She nodded as he gazed at her, his jaw hanging loose in shock. "By court order. I'd gotten into trouble once too often—cheating, drinking, fighting at school. Shoplifting, driving without a license…" Ted's blue eyes grew rounder with every word. "My guardians couldn't control me. The judge ordered me into a rehabilitation program—otherwise I'd have been sentenced to juvenile detention. And so I ended up at Hawkridge."

"Wow." He removed his wire-rimmed glasses and cleaned the lenses with a fold of his shirt. "I had no idea." Replacing them, he took a deep breath. "I guess the program worked, huh? I mean, you're a model citizen at this point. Not to mention a math genius." His grin didn't seem to have changed.

Nola relaxed her weight against the back of the chair. "Hawkridge is a good place. Structured, but caring—they changed my life. If they ask for help, what can I say but yes?"

"I see your point." He stared at his hands, twiddling his thumbs for a moment, then looked up again. "When do you leave?"

"The girls go on spring break this Friday, so I'll arrive the following weekend, before school resumes on Monday."

"Good thing you're free of classes and working on research this term." Ted gave her his usual sunny smile. "Where is this place? Can I visit on the weekends?"

"North Carolina, west of Asheville. In the Great Smoky Mountains."

"On top of ol' Smoky," Ted warbled, putting a painful twang into the words. "That's too far for a weekend jaunt from Boston—except for rich people like you. So you'll be hanging out with these hillbillies until when?"

Nola managed to swallow her irritation at his narrow-mindedness. There was no sense in starting an argument. "Graduation is the first week in June."

He sobered, and reached across the desk to take her hand

in his. "I'm going to miss you, Nola." His thumb stroked across her knuckles. "That's a long time. How about dinner tonight?"

She was glad to think her troubled past didn't bother him. "That sounds good. Where shall I meet you?"

"Why don't we eat in, for a change?" The intensity of his gaze, a certain resonance in his tone, conveyed more than the words. "We can relax, be comfortable."

Nola looked down at their clasped hands. Apparently, he'd decided it was time for them to have sex. Something about her going away had compelled Ted to stake a claim. An hour ago, Nola would have considered that an appropriate next step, too.

An hour earlier, however, she hadn't been thinking about Hawkridge. About Mason Reed.

She manufactured a sudden gasp of surprise and pulled her hand away to pick up her palm computer. "Ted, I'm sorry. I just remembered, I've already set up a dinner meeting with…" She pressed a couple of buttons and discovered she actually did have a dinner meeting scheduled. "With my graduate advisees. Talking over their projects, that sort of thing."

He groaned. "Using mathspeak?"

An old joke between them. Nola smiled. "I'm afraid so."

Ted pushed himself to his feet with a sigh. "As you know, I don't do mathspeak. So I'll let your students have you to themselves." He bent down as if to kiss her cheek, but his lips lingered next to her ear. "I'll call you later tonight, so we can clear the calendar and get together." She expected a kiss, but he flicked her ear with his tongue instead. Then he left her office, whistling.

Wincing and wiping her ear with her sleeve, Nola got up and closed the door behind him, then returned to her desk and recalled the window on her computer. The Hawkridge Web site filled the screen again, with its faculty photograph and list of corresponding names. Among the faces of thirty or so women was one masculine countenance. Mason Reed.

He'd been a first-year teacher during her senior year of high school, advising her as she worked through college applications and acceptances. She hadn't seen him since her graduation day. But the torch she'd carried for him had burned brightly for a long, long time.

"He's a ghost, that's all," she told herself throughout the following week while choosing clothes and packing suitcases. "A phantom from the past. You'll see him, put the memories to rest, then get on with your life. In a few months, you could have a wedding to plan."

Despite her resolution, however, she somehow managed to evade Ted's attempts at seduction every night before she left.

And yet he woke up at 4:00 a.m. on Friday to drive her to the airport. "Don't work too hard," he said in a hoarse voice, looking rumpled and grouchy and sweet all at once.

"I won't." She kissed him, out of guilt and gratitude. "Go home, get back in bed. I'll call you tonight." He backed up several steps, waving feebly, then turned to trudge toward the parking lot.

In the next moment, he'd vanished from her thoughts. Briefcase in hand, Nola headed toward the security checkpoint, already bracing herself for the return to Hawkridge.

Bracing herself for the ordeal of facing Mason Reed.

IN HER DREAM, they sat on a stone wall near the top of the mountain, staring into the mist that cloaked their view of the valley below and talking about colleges she might choose. He'd given her his perspective on the pros and cons, but the choice was hers. Where would she go when she finished high school?

After a long silence, she finally said, "I don't want to leave. I want to stay here." Swallowing hard, she kept her gaze on his face. "With you."

His dark brown eyes widened and he gazed at her for a stunned moment. Then his fingertips touched her cheek.

"Darling…" His southern accent dropped the *g*. "I was afraid to ask. You shouldn't sacrifice a brilliant career for me."

She covered the back of his hand with her palm. "You're all I want. You're all I need."

In the next instant, he pulled her against his chest and took her lips with his. She kissed him back with all her heart, locked her arms around his waist and swore she'd never let him go…

"Ms. Shannon?" An unfamiliar voice wove its way into the scene. "Ms. Shannon? We've arrived."

Nola blinked, then pried apart her scratchy eyelids. "Um…thank you." Her dream vanished like mountain mist under a summer sun, and she was relieved to let it go. Who could spare the time for useless dreams?

Speaking of time, a glance at her watch showed that her appointment with Jayne Thomas, the headmistress of Hawk-ridge, was scheduled for twenty minutes from now. Immediately afterward, Nola would attend her first faculty meeting, which meant she'd be introduced to the other teachers and staff. Some of them were new since her days as a student, but others she knew quite well. Including Mason Reed.

Was he still so charming, so courtly? Would he still make her laugh even while making her think? Maybe he'd gotten fat—or bald. Maybe he was tired, boring, dull.

Or he might still be damn near perfect.

Nola realized her hands were shaking. She gripped them together and stared out the window of her hired car, trying to divert her thoughts with the scenery. All along the winding mountain road, white dogwood flowers fluttered around the tall pine-tree trunks, and patches of purple rhododendron blossoms brightened the dappled shade. Some long-gone gardener had planted drifts of daffodils in the grass at the edge of the forest, and now their cheerful yellow trumpets nodded in the breeze. As a teenager, Nola had spent hours wandering these woods in all seasons and weathers. Judging by today, spring was still her favorite time of year.

The mileage signs on the narrow road up to the school were falling behind, but not fast enough. Nola leaned forward and put her hand on the front seat, but before she could ask the driver to speed up, the car decelerated. In another moment, they'd stopped altogether.

She changed the question. "Is something wrong?"

The driver turned around, looking past her through the rear window. "There's a kid back there on the side of the road."

Nola shifted to follow his gaze. "He's walking oddly. Do you suppose he's hurt?"

"If you don't mind waiting a minute, I'll go and check."

"That will be fine."

The worry on his grandfatherly face eased into a smile. "Thanks."

Nola watched as he walked back down the road. The boy came to a stop as soon as he saw the man approaching. There was a moment of hesitation as they faced each other. Then the driver returned to the car alone.

Nola rolled down her window. "Is he all right?"

Taking off his cap, the man scratched his head. "He's carrying a huge turtle. That's why he's walking strangely."

"A turtle?"

"This big." He rounded his hands, indicating a circle at least a foot in diameter. "But he won't talk to me at all. Won't say a word. Backs away, if I come closer." Smoothing down his thick gray hair, he replaced his cap. "I guess he's been told not to talk to strange men in cars. My kids and grandkids always were."

"Oh." She looked at the boy again, seeing how he struggled to keep hold of the agitated turtle. To judge by the size of that shell, the animal had to be heavy. "Do you think he would talk to a strange woman?"

The driver looked worried again. "I don't…"

A glance at her watch told her they couldn't afford much more delay. "Let's find out." She released the door latch and the driver jumped forward to pull it open for her. Together, they headed toward the boy and the turtle.

The day was warm for March in the mountains, the sunlight strong. A light breeze stirred her hair and cooled her cheeks. Nola stopped about ten feet away from the unlikely pair. "Are you okay?"

He nodded. "Yes, ma'am." Dark, silky hair fell across his forehead and into his brown eyes. His cheeks and arms were pale and freckled, his jeans, shirt and boots, filthy. "Just trying to get this fella home."

The turtle's arms and legs flailed, exposing sharp claws that came close to scratching the boy's hands. Its head and tail poked out and retreated into the shell repeatedly, and with each move the boy was forced to adjust his stance to compensate.

The driver glanced at the forest surrounding them. "Couldn't you just put him down in the woods somewhere along here?"

"I found him down on the highway. He almost got runned over twice before I could pick him up. He needs water and someplace safe. We have a pond out back of the house I think he'll like."

"How far do you have to go?" Nola asked.

"Coupla miles."

"What are you doing so far from home? And on Hawkridge property? This is private land, you know."

"My dad works at Hawkridge. He'll take me and Homer to the pond."

"I've never heard of homer turtles." Nola glanced at the driver, who shrugged.

"Me neither." The boy flashed her an amused look, displaying a deep dimple near each corner of his mouth. "This is *Ter-*

rapene carolina carolina. A common box turtle. Homer's his name. After the Greek poet."

With its black-and-gold patterned shell and wizened, enigmatic face, the creature was, in its own way, fascinating. "How do you know it's a male?"

"Males have red eyes." Closing the distance between them, the boy lifted the turtle toward Nola's face. "See? Females have brownish eyes."

"Ah." She had a feeling he could give her a college-level lecture on the habitat and habits of the box turtle. And she might have been willing to listen, but then she'd be late for her appointment. "Well, if you're okay…" She turned toward the driver. "We should be on our way."

He touched the brim of his hat. "Yes, ma'am." But then he looked at the boy again. In a low voice, he said to Nola, "I hate to leave him alone out here."

Nola looked at her watch again. "He's perfectly safe." She always had been.

The driver wasn't convinced. "Two miles is a long way to walk for a young kid."

She took a deep, calming breath. "You want to give him a ride?"

"If you wouldn't mind, ma'am. Since we're going to the same place."

"Fine." Anything to simply get going. She looked back at the boy. "Would you like a ride to the school?"

He grinned. "Sure!" But then his face fell, as he appeared to reconsider. "Uh… I'm not supposed to ride with strangers."

Nola stared at him, not sure what to do next. "I'm Nola Shannon. I'll be teaching at Hawkridge for the next two months. So I'm not exactly a stranger."

Relief brought out another dimpled grin. "I'm Garrett. If you're a teacher, then it'll be okay." He marched forward, his flailing burden held in front of him. "Let's go. My arms are getting tired."

"You don't want that animal in the car with you," the driver told Nola as they followed the boy. "It's filthy."

She nodded. "We'll put him in the trunk."

With the trunk of the limousine open, however, Nola experienced second thoughts. So, evidently, did the turtle's rescuer. "Homer might get hurt if a suitcase fell on him," he said. "It would be good if we had something safe to put him in." He scrutinized Nola's luggage. "Can we take the stuff outta that little bag and put Homer in there?"

The driver gasped. "Absolutely not!"

But Nola, looking at the boy's worried face, said, "I guess so." *It's just my Louis Vuitton lingerie case.*

With her underwear tucked into a different bag and Homer installed in French leather, she and Garrett got into the backseat. Still shaking his head, the driver restarted the engine and resumed their course.

"Would you like something to drink?" Nola opened the limo's small refrigerator.

"Awesome." The boy sat forward, his eyes wide. "Is this your car?"

"I rented it at the airport. Soda, juice or water?"

He pointed to a can of soda. "Have you got food, too?"

At the touch of her fingers, a sliding panel above the refrigerator revealed crackers, nuts, chips and candy. "Be my guest."

"Oh, wow." He took a bag of chips and scooted back against the seat, munching and sipping. "Where are you from?"

Nola settled into the corner with a bottle of water. "Boston."

Garrett nodded. "I've been there. My mom and dad went to college in Boston. We used to visit sometimes." He stopped chewing, and his gaze turned inward. "She died."

"I'm sorry." Losing a parent was hard, Nola knew from experience—she'd lost both of hers before she was eight years old. But he'd get over it, just as she had.

His shoulders lifted with a deep breath. "My mom liked animals a lot. They have a good zoo in Boston. Have you been there?"

"No, I haven't."

His brown eyes reproached her. "Why not? They have a great zoo in New York, too. And the one in Washington, D.C.—have you been there?" When she shook her head, he stared at her in shock. "Why not? Don't you like zoos?"

"I—I just never think of going, I guess." She'd been to the Boston zoo once on a school field trip, she remembered. And gotten in trouble for climbing into the giraffe enclosure on a dare. The animals hadn't cared, but the chaperones had been furious.

"What do you do for fun?"

"I…" She had to stop and think. "I read and…and do word puzzles." If you could call the *New York Times* crossword a mere puzzle.

"That's all? Don't you go out with your friends or anything?"

"I have a lot of work to do." She didn't want to admit how few people she could call "friend."

Shaking his head, Garrett ploughed into the bag for more chips. "My dad says the same thing. We used to have people over all the time, before…" He sighed again. "He doesn't feel much like seeing anyone these days. Says he's tired."

Nola didn't know what to say, but Garrett didn't seem to require a response, although he did ask politely for another bag of chips. He'd hardly stopped chewing long enough to breathe before the car emerged from the shady forest into bright afternoon sunlight. Just ahead, the road split to form a circular driveway leading up to the front door of the Victorian mansion that housed the Hawkridge School.

Nola chuckled. "I'd forgotten. It looks like a castle, doesn't it?"

Garrett nodded and swallowed at the same time. "Some of the girls call it Hawkwarts. You know, like Hogwarts in the *Harry Potter* books?"

"There is a resemblance." Built by railroad magnate Howard Ridgely in the late nineteenth century, the brick-and-stone house possessed its share of pointed turrets, plus acres of diamond-paned glass in its casement windows and hundreds of feet of iron railing around its porches and balconies. The overall effect should have been forbidding, like the setting for a gothic novel.

But instead, after twelve years away, Nola had the strange impression that she'd been on a long, difficult journey and had now, finally, come home again.

The car stopped beside the entrance. As Nola stepped onto the cobblestone driveway, girls' voices floated through the open doorway from the main hall, competing with the sounds of birds twittering in the trees.

Garrett scrambled out behind Nola and went immediately to the rear of the car. "I need to get Homer to some water."

Lifting the lid of the trunk, the driver said, "I'll bring your bags in, Ms. Shannon. Just have someone tell me where I should put them."

She turned to him and extended her hand. "I will. Thank you for everything. You've been a good sport."

He grinned. "Hey, it's not my suitcase that turtle's been traveling in."

Nola rolled her eyes. "I don't even want to think about it."

Garrett started up the steps, but then hesitated and turned back to wave at the driver. "Thank you for the ride," he said, his cheeks flushed. "Me and Homer woulda had a long walk."

The driver returned a two-fingered salute. "No problem."

Nola joined Garrett on the steps. "Where do you think you'll find your father?"

"In his office or at a meeting or something." The boy picked up Nola's case and climbed the remainder of the stone stairs, leaning a little to the side with the weight of the turtle. "He said he'd be done about four o'clock."

"That gives you at least an hour to wait." As they stepped inside, the tall case clock by the door began to play the Westminster chimes, a sequence as familiar to Nola as her own breath. The huge entry hall—fifty feet square, according to the *Hawkridge Student's Manual*—had always been an afternoon gathering place for students, and nothing had changed there, either. Singles, pairs and groups of girls sat cross-legged on the black-and-white marble floor tiles, leaned against mahogany-paneled walls or perched on the steps of the circular staircase with its wrought-iron banister, studying and gossiping, arguing and laughing, as they'd done for more than forty years.

To the casual observer, the scene suggested a very expensive, very elegant private school for girls. But Agatha Ridgely, Howard Ridgely's only child, had dedicated the estate and her fortune to a special cause. For most of these students, the Hawkridge School was the last resort, a final chance to turn their lives around before their behavioral problems—and the criminal-justice system—took over.

Having rung the chimes, the clock gave three sonorous strikes—marking the time for Nola's appointment with the headmistress. Before the last note died away, a door on the right side of the hall opened. The woman who stepped out smiled as the entry hall instantly went silent.

"It's okay," she said, her voice low but clear. "I won't start cracking the whip until Monday morning at eight."

Judging by their laughter, the girls did not feel particularly threatened.

When she saw Nola, the other woman quickly crossed the floor. She wore a white shirt, dark blue slacks and sensible shoes, but her colorful sweater was decorated with cartoon characters—a crazy rabbit and his roadrunner pal, plus a wise-cracking duck and a bald little man with a rifle.

Her smooth skin revealed she was younger than she'd first appeared. Her chestnut-brown hair, combed back to fell in waves over her shoulders, showed not a single strand of gray.

"Nola, there you are! Welcome to Hawkridge. I'm Jayne Thomas, the ringmaster of this circus. Please forgive the noise—spring break has just ended and the girls are catching up on each other's lives." She took Nola's hand without really shaking it, then looked down at Garrett. "Helping with the luggage, Garrett? That's nice of you."

"Uh, not exactly." He shifted Nola's case to his other hand. "She let me borrow it."

The headmistress widened her eyes. "For what?"

"Homer," Nola said. "A turtle he found on the road."

"Oh, Garrett." The headmistress now looked quite distressed, indeed. "Tell me you didn't put a turtle in that beautiful suitcase."

"He was gonna get hurt in the trunk," Garrett explained. "Ms. Shannon said I could."

"Oh, dear." Jayne Thomas placed a hand on Nola's shoulder. "Garrett's well-known for his collecting habits. He keeps an entire menagerie of injured animals."

"I'm glad I could help." Nola smiled. "I hope his father won't mind one more addition to the collection."

"Dad doesn't care." Garrett glanced up at the curved balcony running around three sides of the entry hall. "There he is now. Dad! Hey, Dad!"

He ran to the circular staircase and started up, lugging the suitcase with him, dodging the girls who lounged on the steps, talking and laughing. "Come see what I found, Dad. It's the coolest box turtle, ever!"

Somewhere out of sight, a man said, "A box turtle, so early in the spring? I guess this warm spell has brought them out of hibernation."

His voice hadn't changed, and Nola would have recognized it anywhere. The years rolled back, and she was eighteen again...

...standing at the foot of the staircase on a hot August afternoon, when a gorgeous guy wearing jeans and a navy sports jacket stepped through the front door. He slipped his backpack off his shoulder, looked in her direction and grinned.

"I'm Mason Reed," he said in a delicious southern drawl. "The new physics teacher. And you are...?"

In love, Nola answered silently. Totally and forever in love. With you.

Chapter Two

"There's Mason, now."

Jayne Thomas's voice brought Nola back to the present. In the next moment, he descended into view on the staircase, but then quickly crouched down to peer at the turtle Garrett—his *son,* Garrett—revealed in Nola's suitcase. Through the iron balusters, she could see that Mason's hair was as dark as she remembered, the same silky brown as Garrett's. Worn a little long, the relaxed waves brushed his jacket collar and the curves of his ears and his eyebrows. Still lean and flat waisted, he straightened up without visible effort.

"Where did the bag come from?" he asked his son as they headed down the stairs. "That's a pretty fancy carrying case for a box turtle."

"I got a ride from the highway," Garrett explained. "It was the coolest car, Dad, with a fridge and a food cabinet and everything. The lady in the car gave me the suitcase."

Mason stopped, braced his hands on his hips and glared at his son. "What have I told you about accepting rides from strangers?" The drawl had hardened, developed a sharp edge.

"It's okay, Dad. She's a teacher." At the bottom of the staircase, Garrett led the way to where Nola stood, paralyzed, beside Jayne Thomas. "See? Ms. Shannon said she'd be working here. With you. So I knew it would be okay."

Nola watched Mason's deep brown gaze widen with shock as he realized who she was. She'd changed her appearance since twelve years ago, but she was still too tall and too thin, with washed-out blue eyes and pale, straight hair.

When he didn't say anything, she swallowed hard and forced herself to smile. "Hello, Mason. It's good to see you again."

"Nola!" The shock in his eyes transformed into pleasure. "Welcome back! I had no idea…" He looked at Jayne Thomas. "Did I know Nola would be teaching here?"

The headmistress shook her head in mock dismay. "There were only about five memos on the topic in your box. She's substituting for Maryann Lawrence during her maternity leave."

Mason winced. "I tend to ignore those. Sorry." Before Nola could prepare herself, he settled his hands on her shoulders and leaned in to kiss her cheek. "That's okay—the surprise is terrific. I'm so glad to see you."

"Thanks." She hoped her voice didn't sound as faint as she felt. He smelled so good, like limes and evergreens and mountain air. His mouth was firm against her skin, his shoulders broad as he came so near.

"And this, I take it," he said, stepping back, "is…*was* your suitcase?" He peered down into the bag, then looked up at her, one eyebrow lifted. "I don't think you'll want it back."

"Um, probably not." She returned his grin with a smile. "Garrett can keep it for collecting purposes."

"Cool," Garrett said. "Dad, I need to get Homer some water. Can I take him to your lab?"

"Sure. Just don't let him loose—the cleaning staff doesn't like wildlife in the hallways."

As the boy went back up the stairs, Jayne Thomas said, "I think that pretty much covers our interview, Nola. I just wanted to say welcome and encourage you to call me with any questions you have. The faculty meeting starts in ten minutes. You remember the way to the library?"

"Of course. Can I tell my driver where to take my luggage?"

"I've put you in Pink's Cottage. I'll have my secretary give him directions and a key."

With a nod, the headmistress went back through the door into the office suite. Nola was aware of all the girls in the entry hall watching her out of the corners of their eyes. For them, this was just the arrival of a new teacher. They didn't know the history behind her meeting—her *reunion*—with Mason Reed.

After an awkward pause, Mason cleared his throat. "You didn't attend the five-year reunion for your class."

"I was at Oxford on a fellowship. I couldn't get back."

He nodded, sliding his hands into the pockets of his jeans. "So I heard. You've made a real success of your career. Not too many mathematicians are close to having Ivy League tenure before they reach the age of thirty."

Nola tried for a light response. "I had a terrific mentor in high school. He helped me believe I could do anything I wanted."

Mason's one-sided smile acknowledged the compliment. "A very smart man." He gestured toward the stairs, walking beside her as she set her feet on steps worn into curves by decades of student use. "I've read your papers. Brilliant, of course. Your Domino corollary, alone, would have secured you a place in the mathematics hall of fame. If there is one."

She gave an embarrassed laugh. "I'm glad there's not."

They reached the top of the stairs and moved into the north wing, along a hallway leading past literature and language classrooms toward the library.

"I have to admit I'm puzzled," Mason said. "Most graduates of Hawkridge send money as their contribution to the school. Very few return to do the work themselves."

He stopped and turned to look at her, his head cocked to

one side. "What really brings you back, Nola Shannon? Why are you here?"

Nola kept her chin up, holding his gaze with her own. But she couldn't answer his question.

Because, at that moment, she couldn't remember what she'd come for—or what she'd planned to do when, after twelve long years, she once again stood face-to-face with Mason Reed.

MASON WINCED as he heard his own words. "And I sound like a nosy old geezer," he said, watching a rosy blush flow across Nola's cheeks. "What I should have said was that I'm really proud of you, and I appreciate your willingness to help out."

The girl he remembered would have stared at the floor in embarrassment. But this new Nola didn't look away, though the tint in her cheeks deepened. "I'm glad. I…I've thought about you often."

He had forgotten the color of her eyes—a pale blue-gray, like shadows on fresh snow. She'd been thin as a teenager and remained so, but the ash-blond hair he remembered hanging halfway down her back was now cut into short, tousled wisps that revealed the shape of her head and set off her delicate pearl-pink ears. The transformation—and his visceral reaction to it—completely confused him.

"I guess the last time I saw you was graduation day." He paused at the door of the library, aware of the teachers inside waiting to meet their new colleague, aware that he wanted to keep her all to himself. "You're not eighteen anymore."

"No." She looked away for a second. "I'm sorry about Ms. Chance… Your wife. Garrett told me."

Mason took a deep breath against the familiar twist in his gut. "That's right. She taught here your last year, didn't she? I wish she had known you better. She was very good for the girls."

Before Nola could reply, a coffee-colored hand with long red, white and blue nails clamped on to her arm.

"Mason Reed," the owner of that hand said, in a loud, rich voice, "you cannot monopolize our new teacher. You bring her in to meet the rest of us right this minute!"

"Alice Tolbert," Mason said, making an introductory gesture toward the short, plump chair of the literature department. "She serves as unofficial faculty den mother."

Alice gave a decisive nod. "Somebody has to keep this crowd in line. Poor Tommy can't do it all herself."

Nola's brows drew together. "Tommy?"

Mason grinned. "That's the girls' nickname for Jayne Thomas. Pretty much everybody calls her Tommy now, though not usually to her face."

"Come on," Alice insisted, drawing Nola after her into the library. "We're all dying to talk to you."

Following Alice and Nola into the library, Mason found a place in the back row of study tables and took a seat. Alice managed to present Nola to every member of the faculty, taking her from group to group with the kind of efficiency an army general would admire. As the headmistress stepped up to the podium, Alice pulled out a chair for Nola at the front table, offered her a notepad and pen, then sat down beside her with an air of satisfaction.

Nola looked shell-shocked, Mason thought, but anybody would, running a gauntlet like the Hawkridge faculty in under ten minutes. Thoughtfully, Jayne made the official introduction her first order of business, and she didn't expect Nola to say anything beyond the standard "glad to be here" before moving right into the business of the meeting.

Mason let his mind wander, but not far for a change. He watched as Nola gradually relaxed her shoulders and spine against the chair, saw her doodling and taking notes. He observed the elegant angles of her elbow and wrist, the graceful crossing and uncrossing of her legs. Gazing at her profile, he saw her lips curve into a smile and caught himself smiling in response.

Damn. He wrenched his gaze from Nola's face to the agenda sheet lying on the table in front of him. The words blurred, focused, blurred again. "Vandalism...spring dance... graduation list..." He should care about these issues.

But all he could think about was Nola Shannon. She'd been a senior when he arrived at Hawkridge for his first teaching position, an orphaned teenager from Boston with a lot of money and no one there who really cared what happened to her. He'd recognized her potential immediately and pushed her toward college, advising her as she prepared the applications. In the process, they'd become friends.

More than friends, to be strictly accurate. In fact, he had almost fallen in love with Nola Shannon.

Fortunately, he'd managed to get control of himself before his job, his career and his good name had been threatened by an inappropriate relationship. The weeks before graduation were always filled with chaos and excitement in equal measure, and he doubted Nola had even noticed how he'd backed off. In a matter of days, it seemed, she'd chosen to attend Harvard, had received her diploma and then—poof— vanished from his life.

Now she was back, and he had a hollow feeling in his belly, as if he'd been tackled by an NFL pro. He hadn't cared about a woman's curves since Gail had gotten sick four years ago, but he sure was noticing Nola's narrow waist, defined by a slim black belt, and the swell of her breasts under a soft gray shirt.

Mason didn't like thinking about a former student this way. As the only male teacher in an all-girls' school, he walked a very narrow line. He'd been careful to keep his balance, since the near miss with Nola. His tutoring sessions always were conducted with at least three girls present, his office door remained open at all times. Any kind of *involvement* with a student, even a former student who'd returned as a fellow teacher, might endanger twelve years of work.

Especially now, when he'd just sent out applications to a dozen different schools across the country, looking for a new job.

More important, he was a man in mourning for his dead wife, with a son who still called out for "Mommy" in his dreams and talked to her when he said his prayers. Garrett wasn't ready to see his father with another woman. Hell, until this afternoon, Mason would have sworn he, himself, wasn't ready to talk to a female about anything more personal than work. Or maybe baseball. Nola's presence didn't— shouldn't—change his situation in the least.

When the meeting finally broke up, Mason left the library without a word to anyone. He would treat Nola as a colleague, keep his distance. Staying current with grading and lesson plans—not that he'd been doing such a great job of that this school year—offered him plenty to occupy his time and his brain. The students needed more than he'd been giving lately. He could improve there, as well. All the while avoiding too much time with the disturbing Nola Shannon.

"So, did you like Ms. Shannon, Dad?" Garrett walked beside Mason on the way home, staunchly carrying Nola's expensive suitcase with its homely occupant inside. "I thought she was cool. She said she went to Hawkridge. Were you her teacher?"

"I was. Back before you were born. Even before your mom and I got married." Which made him feel about a hundred years old—no kind of candidate for a romance, inappropriate or not.

"That must be kinda weird, to see one of your students grown up." Sometimes, Garrett was too perceptive for a ten-year-old. Maybe that happened when kids lost their moms.

"Most students do grow up, you know." Though not always in such an appealing way as Nola had. Mason clenched his jaw, trying not to think about it.

"Yeah." Garrett set down the turtle case in their front yard. "Maybe you could invite her over sometime, so she could see the animals. I bet she'd be interested."

Mason climbed the porch steps and crossed to the front door. "I expect she'll be pretty busy." With the door unlocked, he dropped his briefcase by the table in the hallway. "And I'm pretty busy, too."

"Oh, Dad. You always say that."

"It's always true." Before he could say more, the dogs came running from the back of the house. Gimp, the three-legged terrier mix, made a mad dash for Garrett, his idol, ignoring Mason completely. But Ruff and Ready, two "Carolina brown dog" puppies who'd shown up last winter during a snowstorm, stopped for an ear scratch and a couple of pats before rushing outside to play. Last came Gail's old dog, Angel, a golden retriever with more white than gold in her fur these days and eyes blurred by cataracts. Mason gave her a gentle back rub and some soft words.

"It's *not* always true." Garrett stayed outside on the grass, with Gimp bouncing around him and Homer rustling in the suitcase. "You just don't try anymore. You say you will, but you never do."

When his dad's only answer was a shrug and a crooked smile, Garrett gave up. Blowing a frustrated breath, he picked up the case with Homer inside and headed toward the back of the house and the pond beyond.

At the corner of the house, though, he tried one more time. "Want to come?" he yelled.

"I've got design work to do," his dad answered. "I'll catch you later. Stay out of the water."

The sad thing was, he really did intend to spend time on his airplane plans. Garrett could remember the days when page after page of computer diagrams littered the floor of his dad's office—designs he produced using different systems, materials and structures. He'd built models, too, along with simple balsa-wood planes they used to fly together in the afternoons while Mom cooked dinner.

These days, though, his dad would go into the house, hesitate at the office door, then turn on TV news in the den and sit down with the latest book he'd ordered—always a mystery or science fiction—until dinnertime. Or maybe he'd decide to do some housework. Lately he'd been a real fanatic about keeping everything neat and clean, like Mom always had.

After they ate, Dad would do some grading or make up tests for his classes while Garrett finished his homework. Then they went to bed. His dad didn't go to sleep right away, though. If Garrett woke up in the middle of the night to pee, more often than not his dad was still reading. Or just lying in bed with the light on, staring at the ceiling.

Switching the suitcase from his right hand to his left, Garrett went through the open gate in the backyard fence and on down the slope through the woods leading to the pond. Angel had stayed behind at the house, but Ruff and Ready and Gimp had come with him and now they zigzagged through the undergrowth, checking out scent trails and animal droppings. He'd patrolled the forest this morning, looking for lost baby squirrels and raccoons, grounded birds and other wildlife, so he felt safe letting the dogs run.

The pond filled a small opening amid the trees, with only a narrow bank around it. Sometimes, after a hard rain, the tree roots closest to the pond would be underwater. But today there was a muddy border for him to kneel on as he tipped the case onto its side.

"Okay, Homer. Here you go." He tapped the bottom with his hand. "Slide on out, buddy. This is your new neighborhood."

Homer stuck his head out and looked around, then put one foot on the mud. Gimp came up beside them, sniffing, and Homer jerked back inside his shell.

"Shoo! Go on, Gimp, leave me alone." Garrett pushed the dog away. "Get back in the trees."

Right then one of the other dogs barked, and Gimp took

off to investigate. Garrett encouraged Homer again, and this time the turtle slipped all the way out onto the bank.

Moving carefully, Garrett picked up the bag and backed away, watching to see which way the turtle headed. Homer sat there for a few minutes, then made his slow, steady way toward the high grass along the edge of the water and disappeared.

"Whew." Garrett took a deep breath and let it out. "Stay away from the highway," he said out loud. "You got all you need right here. Prob'ly even a lady turtle to make a family with."

From what he could tell, the instinct to mate and create new members of the species was the major motivation for animals of all kinds. They ate to survive, and they survived to reproduce. That's what his mom had told him.

Garrett glanced up at the patch of pale sky above the pond. "Is that what Dad needs, Mom? A reason to survive?"

His dad cared about him, Garrett didn't doubt it for a minute. But a ten-year-old could take care of himself. Maybe his dad needed a new baby to get interested in. And that would require a mom.

He glanced at the sky again. "I need some help with this, Mom. Show me what to do."

PINK'S COTTAGE, named for the long-departed Josiah Pink, was one of a dozen small houses scattered within walking distance of the Manor, as the main house was called, on the Hawkridge estate. In the grand old days, senior staff members such as Josiah, who had been Howard Ridgely's personal secretary, lived in these cottages. Now the school made ten of these houses available to teachers and kept the other two as guest accommodations.

Nola found her luggage on the floor of the single bedroom in Pink's Cottage, lined up from smallest bag to largest, minus the lingerie case, of course. Fresh daffodils filled a vase on the table by the casement window, cut from the Hawkridge gardens, she was sure. White curtains lifted with the breeze and a white spread stretched invitingly over the plump mattress. She looked forward to settling in there later tonight.

First, there was dinner to get through. Jayne Thomas had caught her at the end of the faculty meeting and invited her to supper in the Hawkridge dining hall. Much as she wanted the chance to relax by herself, an invitation to the head table was not to be declined.

So she spent her free half hour changing for dinner and wondering why Mason had disappeared so fast, without a word or even a wave. The meeting had run long, as the faculty discussed several incidents of vandalism on school property, the upcoming spring dance—the biggest social event of the Hawkridge year—and of course the impending senior graduation. Maybe Garrett was the reason Mason had left so quickly. Maybe they'd gone to the pond together to return Homer to the wild.

Or maybe Mason simply didn't think she was interesting enough to wait around for.

And that was something about Hawkridge that hadn't changed. Twelve years ago, he'd brushed her off like a mosquito at a summer picnic. From an adult perspective, Nola could acknowledge the facts—she'd been a lonely adolescent with a huge crush on a man not much older than herself. Mason had been a teacher with his career and reputation at stake. But at the time...

She knew he cared about her. She saw the glow in his eyes when they talked and laughed. He touched her when they were working together—nothing sexual, of course. Anybody could walk in on them in a classroom. But his hand would rest on her shoulder while he looked over the work on her desk. Or his fingers would brush hers and linger, as he reached for one of the gazillion papers she had to fill out for every college application.

Nola had been with her share of guys, and she could read

the signs. Mason was falling in love with her. Not for her money, like the idiots back in Boston. Mason had a job, and money of his own. And not even just for sex, because any woman would want him if he looked at her twice.

No, Mason wanted her because they were soul mates. Because they were meant to be together, forever. And as soon as she graduated, as soon as she got free of Hawkridge, he would make her his own.

Like most adolescent fantasies, Nola's had been destined to remain unfulfilled. And now, away from the distraction of his magnetic personality, she could remember her resolution regarding Mason Reed. She wanted to put him—her memories and fantasies of him, to be exact—firmly in the past where they belonged. Then she'd marry Ted and have his children, sharing a home and their careers in Boston. They'd spend summers on Cape Cod, or even in France, perhaps, renting a small cottage in Provence. Ted specialized in Napoleonic politics. He could do research while the children learned fluent French.

Unfortunately for her plans and intentions, however, the encounter with Mason this afternoon had simply confirmed Nola's worst fears.

The man appeared to be as irresistible as ever.

Chapter Three

"Why do I have to eat in the kitchen?"

Standing in front of the bathroom mirror, Mason frowned at the knot of his tie, pulled it loose and started again. "Because you aren't old enough to eat at the head table."

"I could eat at one of the girls' tables."

"You don't belong there, either."

"I don't belong in the kitchen." Arms folded, lower lip stuck out, Garrett sat cross-legged on the floor and pouted as hard as he knew how.

"What's wrong with the kitchen?" Mason started over on his tie for the third time. "It's big and warm, and Mrs. Werner lets you eat as much as you want."

"Babies eat in the kitchen."

"I've never seen a baby there. Just you."

"Why can't I stay here by myself?"

Here they went again. "You're not old enough to stay alone."

"I am, too! I'll do my homework, watch some TV. I won't let anybody inside until you get back." He sprang to his feet and threw his arms around Mason's waist. "Please, Dad, please? I'm old enough to take care of myself while you're just over at the school. Please?"

Mason was tempted. Mostly, he was tired of arguing. But

he knew what Gail would say if she were here to be asked. "No, Garrett. I don't feel comfortable leaving you here alone."

"That's stupid." Garrett kicked at the door, slammed it back against the wall and stomped down the hallway to his room. He slammed that door, too.

Mason braced his hands on the edge of the counter and let his head hang, chin to chest. He and Garrett seemed to be flying at different altitudes these days. Nothing much happened without an argument—breakfast, dinner, homework, bath, bed.

As he left the bathroom, he noticed that Garrett's slam had dented the plaster wall behind the door. Mason swore to himself. The house belonged to Hawkridge and he was trying to keep the place intact so he could turn it over to the school without qualms when…if…he left. One more job for the to-do list—repair plaster.

"Come on, Garrett, let's go." He knocked on the closed door as he went by, but got no response. Backing up, he knocked again. "Garrett, don't make this a battle, son. Just do what I ask, please?"

After a long minute, the door opened and a stone-faced boy emerged.

"Thanks," Mason said, putting a hand on one thin shoulder.

His son shrugged off the touch and marched downstairs without a word.

"Get your coat," was a waste of breath. Jaw clenched, Mason slipped into his own jacket, pulled the front door shut and followed Garrett down the porch steps. The only way this day could get worse was if he had to sit beside Nola Shannon during dinner.

Surely fate would not be so cruel.

WITH THE COTTAGE door key in the pocket of her slacks, Nola stepped into the front garden, where rosebushes were leafing out. Early tulips and late hyacinths glowed like jewels in the last rays of spring sunlight. Climbing rose canes rambled through the arched trellis over the gate, as well, and the white picket fence stood in a border of "pinks"—carnations in shades from white to deepest burgundy.

She stopped for a moment, charmed by the pink stucco cottage and its setting. Thankfully, she'd determined how to conquer the challenge Mason's continued appeal presented—all she had to do was keep her distance. She'd taken this sabbatical in the first place to escape the pressure of Ivy League academics, the stress of a publish-or-perish lifestyle, the constant demands on her time and energy from people who always wanted *more*. She could escape at Hawkridge as well as anywhere else, maybe even better.

Long walks in the mountains, good books to read, easy math to teach—those were her goals for the next few months. If she could help some of the students at Hawkridge, then she'd feel her time well spent.

She didn't need Mason's friendship anymore, or his advice. He'd dismissed her when she was eighteen, and she would return the favor now.

Stepping through the garden gate, Nola saw her path was about to merge with that of a young woman approaching with strong, athletic strides. Her hand lifted in greeting as she drew close.

"You're Nola Shannon, right? I'm Ruth Ann Blakely, the riding instructor. Welcome to Hawkridge."

"Thank you." Nola fell into step with Ruth Ann on the cobblestone walk. "It's good to be here. The mountains are so gorgeous this time of year."

Ruth Ann glanced at the hills surrounding them and drew in a deep, appreciative breath. "We're having a really nice spring. I still think fall is my favorite, though. I love the richness of the colors."

"Do you live in one of the cottages?"

The trainer nodded. "Barrett's. It's nearest the stable, done in blues. I hate pink. Are you sitting at the head table tonight?" When Nola nodded, Ruth Ann gave a low whistle. "It's a little unnerving, sitting up there above the rest of the dining hall, knowing everybody's watching and waiting for you to choke on your food."

Nola grimaced. "I hadn't thought about it quite that way."

"Or you could dribble gravy down your front."

"Thanks so much for the suggestion."

Ruth Ann looked her over. "I'm thinking you don't suffer from accidents of that kind, though. Me, I always seem to leave the table with something on my shirt. Last year, the first time I sat at the head table, I dribbled raspberry sauce on my white blouse."

"So you're fairly new to Hawkridge yourself?" They'd reached the paved service road leading to the Manor.

"Yes and no. I only started full-time teaching last fall. But I grew up at Hawkridge, more or less. My dad was the trainer until I took over. My grandfather managed the stable for Howard Ridgely."

"I liked riding," Nola said as they climbed the steps of the east entrance to the house. "Though I wasn't devoted the way some girls were. Still, shouldn't I remember you?"

Ruth Ann opened the heavy mahogany door for Nola to enter. "I groomed and tacked up the horses in the barn and Dad would lead them out for the students to mount. You wouldn't have seen me too often."

She shrugged as she came into the hallway. "But I run my program differently. If you want to ride, you need to know how to take care of the animal. I don't treat these girls like princesses. They may be rich, but they're still human."

Nola winced. "Ouch."

The other woman stopped, thunked the heel of her hand

against her forehead and groaned. "Sorry. Tact is not my strong suit. I didn't mean to insult you. I'm just saying—"

Smiling again, Nola shook her head. "It's okay. Hawkridge has always been criticized for being too exclusive and costing too much. I'm surprised they haven't made some changes by now."

"There are scholarships available nowadays, a few more each year. Miss Agatha was a real snob, though. She's probably turning over in her grave to see the 'lower classes' getting a chance to attend her school."

"It's about time." The paneled doors along this hallway opened into the math and science classrooms. Nola wondered which one would be hers when classes started on Monday. Which one was Mason's?

At the end of the hall they pushed through double doors into the main entry hall and turned right, following a group of girls into the dining hall, once the mansion's ballroom, which occupied the north wing underneath the literature department and the library. Nola caught sight of the students in front of her, dressed in jeans, T-shirts and flip-flops, and leaned close to Ruth Ann.

"No uniforms? They come to dinner in jeans?"

"On weekends," Ruth Ann whispered back. "During the week they have to wear slacks or skirts, nice shirts and proper shoes. Uniforms are for classes only these days."

That would take some getting used to. Nola's Hawkridge uniform hung in one of the closets in her Boston house—a pleated skirt in the sky-blue plaid of the Saint Andrew's clan, to which the Ridgely family was distantly related, along with a white shirt, black sweater and black kneesocks. Maybe she would give away those clothes when she returned home—a personal declaration of freedom.

"I'm sitting with the students," Ruth Ann said as girls filed past them and found their places at the long tables. "I'm advising the girls on Third West this year—all sixth and seventh graders." The dormitory wings at Hawkridge ran east to west, three floors on each side, with twenty-four tenants on each hall. Advisers sat with their students at each meal, rather than at the faculty tables.

"They must give you some trouble, since they're new to the school."

"Oh, they do." The light of battle shone in Ruth Ann's eyes. "But there are twenty horses in my stable, each of them producing fifty pounds of manure a day. Mess with me, I tell them, you'll be moving half a ton of poop before breakfast every morning. Most of the time, they listen." With a wave of her hand, she headed toward the Third West table.

Nola swallowed hard, squared her shoulders and made her way down the long center aisle to the head table. On either side, she felt the curious gazes of the girls, heard whispers running along the tables. There was surveillance, as well, from the dining-hall staff setting out food, and from those teachers already seated on the dais. She couldn't see them clearly, and although she kept walking, the head table seemed to recede with each step, until she began to think she would never arrive. By the time she reached it, she wondered if trial by fire wouldn't have been easier.

Jayne Thomas was waiting for her. "Thanks for coming." She put one hand on Nola's back and motioned her forward with the other one. "I know that's a tough walk, but it is a Hawkridge tradition. I've put you on my right, with Mason Reed on your other side. You can relax now."

Hah, Nola said to herself. *That's what you think.*

Mason stood up as she approached, and pulled out the chair she would sit in. Tonight, he wore a navy blazer and tan slacks, with a white shirt and the Hawkridge tie—burgundy with a golden hawk's head pattern. His smile seemed stiff, even distant, and his dark eyes somehow missed connecting with hers.

Still, a peculiar kind of vibration hummed through her body at the sight of him. Nola didn't know whether she was going to faint or be sick. She was pretty sure she wouldn't be able to eat a bite.

But she managed some kind of smile. "Hello, again."

"Welcome to dinner." He slid the chair in behind her as she sat down, catching her behind the knees at just the right moment. Then he took his seat beside her. "You handled that quite well."

She reached for the water goblet at her place and took a much-needed drink. "I wish I'd been warned. I didn't remember it as such an ordeal."

Mason shook out his napkin. "The girls never do realize. But it's basically the final test before you get the job."

Nola surveyed the crowd rather than look into his face. "Has anyone ever failed?"

"I once saw a prospective teacher break down and run out," he said. "A couple of years after you left, I'd guess that was. He never returned."

"He?" She lifted the goblet again, watching the play of light through the cut crystal. "What was *he* supposed to teach?"

He hesitated for a pregnant moment. "Self-defense."

She'd just taken another sip of water. Stunned by Mason's dry delivery and unbalanced by her own nerves, Nola laughed so suddenly and so hard that she sprayed water over her plate, the tablecloth and the front of her shirt.

A single second earlier, Tommy had rung the bell signaling the start of the meal. An immediate silence fell, exposing Nola's indecorous sputter to the entire crowd.

Under the table, Mason handed her his napkin to wipe her dripping chin. Tommy glanced their way, but kept a straight face. "Students and faculty of Hawkridge School, welcome back from your spring travels. The staff and faculty are glad everyone's returned safely, and we look forward to getting down to work again. For now, however, enjoy your meal."

After a brief round of applause had died away, Mason said, "Salad?"

Her gaze fixed on her plate, Nola shook her head. "No, thank you."

Dark green spinach leaves, golden orange slices and huge walnut pieces tumbled onto her plate from the spoon in his hand. "It's okay," he said quietly. "Nobody noticed."

"Of course they did," she hissed. "The entire dining room saw me make an utter idiot of myself."

"They saw you being human."

She snorted, but didn't speak. When the baked chicken and wild rice came Mason's way, he served Nola, then himself. "You'll get more attention if you don't eat something," he told her.

She picked up her fork, searching for a diversion of some kind. "Where is Garrett having dinner?"

"In the kitchen with the staff. They're all practically family."

Her first bite of the chicken awakened a cascade of food memories. "Mrs. Werner is still the cook?" Forgetting to be wary, she stared at Mason in surprise. "I always thought she would retire any minute. She must be in her seventies now."

He nodded, smiling. "She brought in her daughter to help. And her granddaughter lends a hand for big occasions."

The bread basket arrived. Nola unfolded the cloth and inhaled deeply. "Oh, they make the same rolls as when I was here. How wonderful!" She placed one roll on her plate, hesitated, then took another.

Beside her, Mason chuckled. "That's the first enthusiasm I've seen you exhibit since you arrived."

She tore off a piece and closed her eyes to savor the yeasty, buttery flavor. "I used to steal them," she confessed. "I'd gather as many as I could get away with and put them in my shirt, under my sweater. After lights-out, I'd have this orgy of roll eating. They were so warm, so sweet—"

"Is that your best memory of Hawkridge School, then? The dinner rolls?"

The question seemed casual enough. Just in time, though, Nola recognized the easy familiarity that had sprung to life between them. She'd promised herself she wouldn't fall under the spell of his grin, wouldn't allow herself to be enchanted by his warm, intimate drawl. She didn't need Mason Reed anymore.

So she would turn the tables on him. "I'd forgotten that about you," she told him, spearing her fork into crunchy spinach and a juicy slice of orange.

"Forgotten what?"

"That you're always asking questions, always poking and prodding, getting people to think, to reveal details they hadn't planned to share."

When she glanced at him, he was staring at her with his dark eyes round, his brows lifted. "I do that?"

"Don't try that innocent face with me. You know you do it quite deliberately."

"But you didn't answer the question."

"My favorite thing about Hawkridge…" She looked out over the dining hall, at all the girls settled in to eat, at the teachers sitting with them, keeping an eye out for any trouble, at the quiet, caring servers, mostly women, moving among them. At that moment, one of the staff set a bowl of ice cream and a steaming apple pie on their table, just to Mason's right.

Confessing the truth would make her vulnerable. She had to stay strong, keep him at a distance.

"My favorite thing at Hawkridge," Nola said firmly, "was always dessert."

AFTER DISMISSING the girls from the dining hall, Tommy turned to Nola and Mason. "I'm having a few people in for drinks. Please come, both of you."

Nola hesitated, but Mason did not. "Thanks," he said,

keeping his eyes on the headmistress, "but I think I'd better get Garrett home. He's supposed to show up for a soccer game out in town at eight tomorrow morning."

"So he is on a team?" Tommy asked. "I wasn't sure you'd convince him to try out."

Mason shrugged. "I can't always get him to go to practice, which means he doesn't get much chance to play. I'm hoping a few games spent sitting on the bench will change that behavior."

Tommy nodded. "Well, good luck." She turned to Nola. "Professor Shannon, can you join us?"

At that moment, Mason lost the battle to keep his gaze away from Nola Shannon. Her fair hair shone silver in the lights of the dining-hall chandeliers. She wore solid black—a shirt and slacks Mason thought were silk, and a jacket he knew was cashmere from the feel of it when he'd helped her put it on after the meal. He'd managed the process without actually touching her at all. Too bad he hadn't held his breath, and so would have to remember the drift of expensive perfume he'd caught when she was close.

Then she shook her head in response to Tommy's invitation. "I'm very grateful, but I flew out at six this morning and haven't really caught my breath since then. Could I take a rain check?"

"Of course. I should have realized." Tommy put her hand on Mason's arm. "Your way goes past Pink's Cottage. Be sure Nola gets home safe, won't you?"

Not exactly what he'd intended, but at least Garrett could chaperone. "Sure."

Tommy walked with them to the kitchen to give Mrs. Werner her compliments on the dinner, and then left for her own quarters in the main part of the Manor. Garrett sat at the big oak table in the center of the huge Victorian kitchen, finishing up a giant-size dish of apple pie and ice cream.

He ignored Mason, but his eyes lit up when he saw Nola. "Ms. Shannon! I got Homer down to the pond this afternoon. He slipped right into the grass like he belonged there."

"I'm glad he felt at home," Nola said. "I'm sure he was grateful to you for taking care of him."

"Unlike some children," Mason muttered to himself. More loudly, he said, "Finished, Garrett? We need to get home."

Picking up the bowl, Garrett proceeded to slurp down the last of the melted ice cream.

"Garrett." He closed his eyes in shame. "That's rude."

Slurp.

"I try," Mason told Nola. "But he's a boy."

She smiled. "A suitable explanation." Glancing around the room, Nola shook her head. "I spent more than my share of time in here. Whenever I made trouble—and I made a lot of trouble in the first couple of years—a teacher would assign me kitchen duty. I developed into a terrific potato peeler."

"That you were." Mrs. Werner set a wide ceramic bowl covered with a cloth on the table. "Did you like my rolls tonight, Miss Nola?"

Before Nola could answer, the cook tugged her into a hug. Caught in the ample embrace, Nola's slender body remained stiff. After a moment, she lifted a hand and patted the cook's shoulder, then drew back, putting a good distance between them.

"Of course," she said, cheeks pink, voice shaky. "Those rolls are even better than I remembered."

"You should take a few with you." Mrs. Werner turned to one of the cabinets. "I always have leftovers."

"No, really…" But Nola's voice died away as she was handed a paper package. "Thank you," she said, blushing yet again. "I'll enjoy them, I know."

Mason pulled Garrett's chair away from the table, then scooted it back in when his son stood up. "We'll get out of your way," he told Mrs. Werner. "'Night."

"More rolls in the morning," Mrs. Werner told Nola. "Come for breakfast."

They left through the kitchen door and turned west, toward Pink's Cottage. "I'll need a new wardrobe when I leave here," Nola said. "I'll have gained fifty pounds eating these rolls."

"You'll get your share of exercise," Mason said, watching Garrett sprint ahead of them. "The faculty still plays volleyball on Mondays and Wednesdays. You can join them."

"I haven't played in years," she said. "I remember the student/faculty game my senior year, though. You spiked the ball practically down my throat. Scared me to death."

Mason grinned. That had been a great hit. "The students won anyway."

"Are you still playing?"

The answer wasn't easy to give. "When Gail…" He cleared his throat. "There's not as much time as there used to be. I don't play anymore, either."

"That's too bad." Her hand lifted as if to touch his arm, then fell back at her side.

They walked the rest of the way to her cottage in silence, with six feet of cool night air between them. When Mason opened the Pink's Cottage garden gate, Nola stepped through, then turned to face him, closing the white picket panel between them.

"Thanks for the escort."

"My pleasure." His pleasure, indeed. The night's shadows showed off the arches of her cheekbones, the squared curve of her chin, the provocative fullness of her lower lip. Mason made himself look away from Nola's mouth and found himself caught in the glimmer of her pale eyes, shining almost silver in the darkness. She stood just a breath or two away, protected only by the flimsy barrier of the picket gate. A kiss would be so easy to give…to take….

"Hiiii*yah!*" Garrett yelled from somewhere behind him, battling imaginary aliens with his own brand of martial arts.

Nola jumped, and took a step backward. "He's quite a handful. And a charmer to go along with it. I didn't know children could be so easy to talk to."

"Oh, yes." Mason scrubbed a hand over his face, hoping to clear his brain. "Until you say no. Then he turns into the Incredible Sulking Child."

Since sunset, the breeze had picked up, become an actual wind. Clouds veered across the sky, obscuring the stars, veiling the moon. "Here comes our rainy weather."

Nola shivered inside her sweater. "But today was so beautiful!"

Mason rejected the urge to put himself between her and the cold. "The mountains are unpredictable. We've had snow-storms later in the spring than this. Hope you brought your raincoat and boots." He glanced over his shoulder and called, "Come on, Garrett, let's go."

Even as he looked back toward Nola, he heard the door to Pink's Cottage shut tight. The lock clicked into place. She'd gone inside without saying goodbye. He only wished he felt relieved.

Garrett ran up and tackled him around the waist. Apparently, all was now forgiven. "Where's Ms. Shannon?"

"In her house, where we should be." A Freudian slip, if ever there was one. "I mean, we should be in our house."

His son didn't notice the mistake. "I was gonna ask her to come over tomorrow to see the pond and the animals."

Close call. Mason sighed. "Right now, you need to go to bed, get ready for your soccer game tomorrow."

"Aw, Dad, do I hafta play?" Garret dropped his arms and trudged on alone, his head hanging low. "I don't like the guys on the team. And the coach is mean. Can't I stay home?"

Back to the old routine, Mason thought, blanking out the memory of Nola's mysterious gaze in the moonlight. *Thank God.*

Chapter Four

Mason's weather prediction proved drearily accurate. A sharp rain fell all day Saturday, and the outside temperature barely reached fifty degrees. With a well-stocked kitchen and a cord of wood for the fireplace right outside the back door, Nola felt no desire to stir from her cozy cottage. She got down to work, instead, using the lesson plans and notes from the teacher she'd replaced to prepare herself for her Monday-morning classes. Mathematics always filled her mind to the exclusion of everything else, so she didn't think about Mason more than once…an hour.

The rain continued through the night and into Sunday morning. When she looked up from her papers around three in the afternoon, however, she saw sunshine glittering in the drops of water on the new leaves outside her window. Sticking her head out the door, she found the air brisk but not unbearable, especially since she'd just lived through one of the coldest winters on record for Boston.

So she pulled on the boots she had, in fact, brought with her, buttoned her raincoat over her sweater and set off for a walk in the wake of the storm.

She paused at the garden gate, remembering Friday night. For a moment, she'd thought Mason was going to kiss her.

And for that moment, she'd certainly wanted him to. He'd kissed her on the cheek earlier that afternoon, and she'd loved the smoothness of his lips against her skin. How would it feel to have his mouth on hers?

But then he'd turned away to call Garrett and she'd taken the chance to escape before she did something stupid, like throwing herself into his arms. The man was dangerous. He should be avoided at all costs.

As Mason and his son had walked away, though, she'd watched through her cottage window. Wherever they lived, they'd continued in a westerly direction, past her cottage and on toward the woods.

For her Sunday walk, Nola headed due east.

Girls were emerging from the dormitory, most of them in groups, chattering with the energy of those who'd been confined inside too long. Several girls wore breeches and carried helmets, clearly planning a ride at the stables. As Nola passed the athletic fields, on the north side of the Manor, volleyballs were being batted around and tennis balls smacked against a backboard at one end of the courts. Runners jogged past her, giving a nod or a slight wave when she smiled. Hawkridge had always encouraged exercise as a way of releasing tension and lifting a bad mood. Nola supposed that was why she was out walking, herself.

She reached the head of Hawk's Ridge Trail about half an hour after she left her cottage. By taking this path, she left the civilized portion of the school behind and stepped into wilderness—an old-growth forest full of trees whose lives spanned centuries. High above her head, spring leaves had just emerged. Nola wondered if anyone had been this way since last summer, since the fallen leaves from autumn still lay flat and wet on the trail.

She set as her goal the farthest point on Hawkridge property from the Manor, a walled overlook on the edge of the mountain. The path ran downhill to that point and then circled back. She could return the way she'd come or continue by the longer route, but either way would be a steady uphill climb. She'd see how she felt when she got there before deciding which way to go.

Nola slowed her steps and finally halted to gaze across the clearing at the wall on the side of the mountain—the wall where she embraced Mason in her dream.

But she'd never been in this place with Mason. That embrace had never happened, no matter how many nights she had lain in her lonely dormitory bed wishing it would. As for the dream, Nola considered it a reminder that she really needed to put the infatuation with Mason behind her, so she could move into the future with Ted.

Crossing to the wall, she looked over the valley below, seeing spring greens of every description in the treetops, a church spire here and there, the flash of water in the French Broad River. Bright sunlight streamed from a cloudless sky and a fresh breeze carried the scents of pine and earth.

And cigarette smoke.

Nola turned just as a girl came down the path, cigarette dangling from one hand. She had to be from Hawkridge, but smoking by students was strictly forbidden. Teachers were expected to enforce the rule and encouraged to abstain, themselves.

Nola swallowed hard, lifting a hand in greeting as the girl stepped into the clearing. "Good afternoon."

After a long drag on the cigarette, the girl sauntered to the wall and sat down. "Hey."

Her thick, curly hair was pulled into a bouncy tail on the crown of her head. All of her clothes were too big—baggy black sweatpants, a baggy black T-shirt and some kind of military-style jacket in desert-camouflage colors—and her shoes seemed to be black military boots.

But her face was feminine and lovely, with dark almond-shaped eyes, golden skin and a full, red mouth.

Taking a seat for herself on the other end of the wall, Nola cleared her throat. "I'm Ms. Shannon. I'll be teaching math."

The girl nodded. "Yeah. I have you second period."

"What's your name?"

"Zara." Another drag, and a smoke ring. "Kauffman."

"I'm glad to meet you, Zara." When the girl didn't answer, Nola said, "You know smoking isn't allowed anywhere on the school grounds."

Zara heaved a melodramatic sigh. "Technically, I'm not on the grounds. This overlook sticks out about fifteen feet from the side of the mountain." She sent Nola a mocking smile. "Cantilevered, as in." She tossed the last of the cigarette into the valley below.

Jaw set, Nola got to her feet. "And a piece of paper wrapped around tobacco doesn't qualify as litter when you throw it on the ground?"

Now the girl rolled her eyes. "Jeez. Chill, why don't you? It's just a butt."

"It's trash. If you have to indulge in such a filthy habit, at least have the decency to dispose of your litter properly." She started back the way she'd come, wanting to put distance between herself and Zara as quickly as possible.

"Hey," the girl called after her. "Are you going to chit me?"

Nola stopped and considered. She hadn't thought about the practice of writing up a chit to report a student's misbehavior in quite some time, even though she'd certainly received her share. Pivoting, she shoved her hands into her coat pockets. "Is there some reason I shouldn't?"

Zara came toward her. Nola realized the girl was almost as tall as she was, and probably heavier.

She stopped within arm's distance. "That's not very nice."

"Smoking isn't very nice." Nola fought the urge to back away. "The headmistress will want to talk to you about it, I'm sure."

The almond-shaped eyes narrowed to slits. "You make trouble for me, I could make trouble for you."

Nola laughed. "You could try. I wouldn't advise it, however."

"Yeah, well, we'll see who's laughing tomorrow in class."

The girl barreled past, deliberately ramming her shoulder into Nola's chest and knocking her to the side. Nola grabbed a tree trunk to keep from losing her balance. When she looked beyond the tree, she saw that the ground fell sharply away at that point. If Zara's shove had been just a little harder, she could have taken a nasty, even fatal, fall.

"Welcome to Hawkridge," she muttered, starting the long trek back to campus. "Enter at your own risk!"

THE MATH-AND-SCIENCE hallway was still quiet when Nola arrived at seven-thirty Monday morning. She stepped through the open doorway of the classroom Jayne Thomas had assigned her when they'd talked on the phone the day before, and flipped three switches to turn on the lights. Two columns of tables faced the front of the room, with two chairs at each table.

Putting her books and bags down on the teacher's desk facing the students, Nola noted yet another change at Hawkridge—the blackboard she'd expected to find had been replaced by a white erasable surface. She realized she missed the faint scent of chalk in the air, part of the atmosphere she associated with her high-school years.

As she wrote her plans for the day at one end of the board, with a felt-tipped marker, someone spoke from the doorway. "That looks official."

She whirled to find Mason leaning a shoulder against the door frame, his hands tucked into the pockets of his jeans, one foot crossed over the other. He looked exactly as she'd remembered him all this time, relaxed and confident, with a slight smile curving his lips and a friendly glint in his eyes. He wore soft leather loafers, a chambray shirt with a narrow green tie loosened at the neck and a brown corduroy jacket. His hair was mussed, as if he'd already raked his hand through it several times. The sight of him took her back to a different classroom, where…

She'd snagged her usual desk, in the far corner on the last row, and was just taking her seat when the new physics teacher came through the door. Complete silence reigned as all the girls sat with their mouths open, staring in awe.

Nola thought she might die of happiness when he glanced at her across the heads in between them, winked and grinned. The girls in the row ahead of her twisted around to glare with open round eyes and eyebrows raised in question. Nola just smiled. Sierra Brown stuck out her tongue. Then everyone faced forward as their hunky new teacher cleared this throat.

"Good morning," he drawled, leaning his hips back against the desk and crossing one foot over the other. "I'm Mr. Reed and I'll be teaching physics this year."

A sigh breezed through the room as the girls took in his dropped g's and soft vowels.

"And, yeah, this is my first teaching job ever. I graduated from Harvard, in Cambridge, Massachusetts, last spring. A friend of mine—Ms. Chance, that would be—teaches biology here at Hawkridge. She let me know you needed a physics teacher, and so here I am."

The girls sighed again as he made two-syllable words out of "here" and "am."

"Physics has a reputation for ruining grade point averages," he told them, grinning, "but it's a lot of fun when you get the hang of it. I'll be holding help sessions here in my classroom on Tuesday and Thursday afternoons. I'll also be available to work with students individually, and there's a sign-up sheet on my office door for that purpose. I'm hoping to get to know all your names over the next couple of weeks,

but forgive me if I start out pointing at you if there are questions. There will be homework every night..."

"Nola?"

Jerked out of her memories, Nola cleared her head with a hard shake. "Um, g-good morning."

"Are you ready for your first dose of Hawkridge hellions?"

She widened her eyes. "You call them that?"

Mason winced and glanced over his shoulder. "Not so they can hear. In reality, they're not bad overall. They will be hard to handle today, though, coming down off vacation."

"Did you call me that when I was a student?"

His smile faded as his shoulders lifted on a deep breath. He shook his head. "I was a lot younger then, idealistic. I thought I would be able to make a real difference in the lives of the girls at Hawkridge."

She took a step toward him. "You do! You did for me. I doubt I would have gone to college, or even graduated from high school if you hadn't worked with me and shown me what I could accomplish."

Mason nodded. "You are one of the big success stories, no doubt about it. Hawkridge does have its star graduates, of course. And a few spectacular failures—a department-store heiress famous simply for being famous comes to mind, an actress notorious for her binge drinking and, oh, yeah, a senator's wife recently indicted for running an escort service."

Nola let her jaw drop. "*She* went to Hawkridge?"

"Along with a lot of average young women who now lead relatively normal lives."

"That is a success for many of them," she reminded him.

He straightened up, rubbing a hand over his face. "Sure. I guess I'm just tired. Garrett woke up with a fever Saturday morning that turned into the flu. He doesn't sleep well when he's sick, so neither do I."

She couldn't imagine taking care of a sick child by herself. "Is he better today?"

"Not well enough for school, but he's doing okay."

"Is someone staying with him at home?"

"He's in the infirmary for the day, with Nurse Ryan. That way I can check on him between classes and at lunch."

"She's still here, too?"

Mason chuckled. "I think she's actually part of the building." Then he yawned and rubbed his eyes, just as the warning bell for classes rang. "Time to get to work. I hope your day goes well."

"Thanks. You, too."

He lifted his hand and eased out of the doorway just as the first students arrived. They wore uniforms this morning—the same blue plaid she'd worn, in an updated, A-line style, with white shirts and black sweaters. Black tights had replaced kneesocks, but every girl's hair was still neat, every face scrubbed clean.

"Good morning," she said when the final bell sounded. "I'm Ms. Shannon. I'll be replacing Mrs. Lawrence for the rest of the school year. We're picking up right where you left off before spring break, with integrals and matrices. If you'll turn to page 233 in your books, we'll start by looking at some of the sample problems."

Nola faced the board, wrote page 233 at the top, and then copied an equation from the page. When she turned toward the students again, a glint on her desk caught her eye.

She looked down. Someone had set a tall glass of water just in front of her desk chair, and had placed a large white linen napkin beside it. An obvious reference to her faux pas at dinner Friday night.

She looked at the students, all of whom appeared to be concentrating on page 233 in their books—except for the grins they couldn't quite stifle. What reaction did they expect?

Nola picked up the glass and toasted the class. "To our first day together." She took a long drink and blotted her lips with the napkin. "Thanks. Now, let's review the characteristics of a matrix. The standard form is…"

Forty minutes later, the bell rang to end the first period. The girls rushed out. Nola sank into her desk chair and propped her head on one hand. She'd talked the entire time. Not a single student had asked a question or answered her when she asked one. Maybe they all understood the subject. Or maybe they just wanted to make her as uncomfortable as possible.

She straightened and stood up as her second-period algebra students arrived. Zara Kauffman sat down in the last row, at the corner farthest from the front of the room, and leaned forward to talk to the girls beside and just in front of her. When the bell rang, they were still talking.

"Good morning," Nola said, pitching her voice for the back row to hear her. "Let's get started with class. I'm Ms. Shannon." She repeated her introductory statement. Zara and her friends paid no notice.

"Zara, I need your attention, please." When the girls continued to ignore her, Nola walked to the back of the room. "Girls, class is beginning. Face the front, please, so you will be able to see the board."

The two girls at the table ahead of Zara slowly swiveled in their seats. But Zara and her tablemate continued to talk.

"Zara!" She made her voice harsh and loud, a method she'd never used in her college classes. "Stop talking. Now."

The girl rolled her eyes. "Yes, ma'am," she said with an ugly sneer on her face. "Whatever you say, ma'am."

Nola nodded. "Thank you." She moved toward the front of the room, beginning her lecture as she went. "From Mrs. Lawrence's notes, I see that your class has been working with quadratic equations. If you'll open your books to page—"

She stopped walking and talking as she glanced at her desk. A new glass of water had joined the one left by the first-period class. A new napkin lay beside it.

Now it was her turn to take a deep breath. Going to her desk, Nola picked up the new glass and again toasted the students. "Thanks." She took a sip, blotted her mouth and continued with the lesson—forty minutes of nonstop uninterrupted mathematics.

By lunchtime, after four classes and four glasses of water, plus more student resistance than she'd have believed possible, Nola decided that Hawkridge girls could teach the Ivy League a thing or two about stress.

JAYNE THOMAS CAUGHT Mason's arm as he walked past her in the hall after fifth period. "Have you seen Nola since classes started?"

He shook his head. "I ate lunch with Garrett in the infirmary." Thereby avoiding any chance of encountering the woman in question.

"I've scheduled a conference on Zara Kauffman after school," Tommy said quickly. "And I need the two of you to attend. Could you bring Nola to the conference room about three-fifteen?"

"Sure." The headmistress moved on with the flow of students in the hallway, but Mason stood still for moment. If he didn't know better, he'd think Tommy was conspiring to get him together with Nola. Or was that just wishful thinking?

He'd felt compelled to welcome her this morning, but that should be the extent of his hospitality. The location of her classroom, on the opposite side of the math/science hallway from his and at the far end, excluded all possibility of a wave, a smile or a brief hello during the changes of class. He was grateful for the reprieve.

Once sixth period ended, though, he packed up his briefcase and made the walk toward the door into the entry hall. Nola's classroom was the first on the right.

Bracing himself, he knocked on the door and then stepped inside. "How'd it go today?"

She stood where he'd found her this morning, only now she was erasing the board instead of writing on it. This time, she didn't turn to look at him.

"Okay." With great precision, she eliminated every trace of writing on the white surface. "The girls were a little… um…reserved. We'll get past it."

Mason noted the collection of glasses on her desk. "Looks like you had a party. I wasn't invited?"

Nola ran her free hand through her hair. "Each class managed to surprise me by putting a glass of water and a napkin on the desk. Just a little reminder of my Friday-night gaffe."

She looked at him then, and he saw the blaze of embarrassment in her cheeks. "The first time was fairly clever. By the fifth, I'd lost my sense of humor."

"I'm sorry. I told you they were tough."

"Yes, you did. I don't know if I'll be able to teach them anything—they don't ask questions and they don't respond to mine."

Mason couldn't resist stepping close enough to put a comforting hand on her shoulder. He immediately regretted it when her sophisticated scent wrapped around him, a distraction if ever there was one.

"Give them a few days," he suggested. "They have to test the new teacher, see what the limits are. If you hold your ground, they'll be the ones to back down. I went through the same thing."

"Are you kidding me?" She laughed, even as she moved to put the width of the teacher's desk between them. "You walked in and every girl in every class was smitten with an undying crush. You had us all eating out of your hand by the end of the day. Believe me, I know."

As he gazed at her in surprise, the blush on her cheeks stained her throat, as well. "Forget it," she muttered, cramming papers into a leather tote. "I've got to get started on grading homework."

Mason blinked hard, searching for his voice. "Uh, first, Tommy wants us to join her for a conference." He glanced at the clock on the back wall. "About five minutes ago."

Nola blew out a short breath. "Then we'd better show up." With the bag in her hand swinging a wide arc, she left the room and strode quickly down the hall. Mason flipped off the light switches and followed in her wake.

He caught up at the door from the entry hall into the administrative offices, just as Alice Tolbert stopped Nola to ask about her first day of classes. Nola made the experience sound like a vacation instead of the trauma she'd described to him.

"Sounds like our girl is settling in," Alice said to Mason as he passed by. "Maybe we can convince her to come back next year?"

Mason managed a noncommittal smile and followed Nola into the office. He thought Hawkridge might be lucky if she agreed to come back next week.

The conference-room door was open. From the head of the table, Jayne Thomas motioned them in. "Have a seat." She gestured to two chairs beside her own. "Mason, you'd better close the door. I don't want to be overheard."

That didn't sound good. Mason did as requested, then took the chair to Nola's right. "What's going on?"

"I spent the weekend reviewing academic records for the senior class," the headmistress said, pulling several folders out of the stack in front of her. "We have five students who stand in danger of not graduating because of poor grades. Zara Kauffman is one of them."

When Nola gasped, Mason looked at her. "Did she give you trouble today?"

"A little." She shrugged. "Also, I met her at the Hawk's

Ridge Overlook Sunday. She was rude. And she defied me when I cautioned her about smoking."

Jayne shook her head. "We'll have to deal with that. I've scheduled this conference because we need to work on Zara from all angles—academic, behavioral and emotional. Nola, I think you've met all our teachers, but let me introduce Sharon Duff, our therapist." Sharon, a slim, dark-skinned woman with a gentle smile, waved at Nola. "She's new to the staff since your time. Alice teaches Zara in senior English lit, Jan Alvarez has her for Spanish and Kathy Burns is our art teacher. The only course Zara deals with successfully is advanced art."

"She's quite good," Kathy said. "I'd like to see her go into a college program, but she won't cooperate."

"If she doesn't graduate, she won't get into anything but a dead-end job." The headmistress glanced at Nola and Mason. "She's failing algebra and physics outright. I want Zara to receive tutoring for the remainder of the year. Let's get those grades up enough to send her away with a high-school diploma."

Mason leaned forward, his elbows resting on the arms of the chair. "I've talked to her repeatedly about attending my afternoon help sessions. She simply doesn't come. I can't go to her room and drag her out."

"No, but *I* can. And if I have to become her personal escort, I will. Sharon will work with Zara on that in her counseling sessions, which will be mandatory. I'd prefer not to embarrass the girl by making her situation widely known, however. I want you to work with her one-on-one."

When he held up a hand, Tommy said, "I know. You don't do private sessions with the girls. That's why I'm including Nola in this conversation. I'm sure she's able to tutor Zara in physics as well as math.

"I want the two of you to work together and come up with a plan of study. Your collaboration is required if Zara is going to graduate in June."

Chapter Five

Nola said, "But…" When Tommy looked at her, she cleared her throat. "Zara already dislikes me. She was outright defiant today in class. I don't think she'll listen to a word I say."

The headmistress stared into space for a minute, thinking. "Okay, then maybe Mason should attend the sessions, too, at least in the beginning. He has a way of persuading girls to learn in spite of themselves," she said with a wink at Nola. "As you probably remember."

She sat down and folded her hands on the stack of files. "I'll talk to Zara this afternoon and make her understand that she doesn't have an option regarding the counseling or the tutoring. She will attend, or she'll be sent home." Her face softened. "And I'm afraid the one thing Zara dislikes more than school is living with her family. Sharon, can you share some of your insights on Zara?"

For the next fifteen minutes, Sharon filled them in on Zara's history of rebellion against a family who valued her far less than her four brothers. Zara's outrageous behavior at home—sneaking out, promiscuity, drinking and drug use, car theft—had been a demand for attention.

"I suspect she's looking ahead now and feeling scared," Sharon told them. "Her family is wealthy, and she's been sheltered from the real world. What's she going to do when she leaves Hawkridge? She's been pretty antisocial here, too, but at least we take care of her and she knows there's a support system in place. Once outside our gates she won't have that, even at home. Perhaps she's failing because she hopes she can stay another year."

"But we can't hold her over," Jayne said. "You only get one chance to graduate at Hawkridge. She must succeed."

"Must *want* to succeed," Sharon added.

After some additional input from Eloise and Alice, the conference came to an end. Nola left the room quickly, but this time she waited for Mason in the hall. They couldn't discuss Zara in front of all the girls hanging around, so they walked in silence until they'd left the building by the door at the end of the math-and-science hallway.

"I don't see how this will work," she said in a low voice, when they couldn't be overheard. "Zara made it plain this morning that she wouldn't concede one ounce of cooperation to me."

Mason had his own reservations, but for entirely different reasons. How was he supposed to work so closely with Nola and remain impervious? "I can tutor her in math and physics. That's not a problem. But I don't usually hold private sessions with the girls." Surely he wouldn't have to explain why, to Nola of all people. She would remember.

They were working in his office after school, trying to finish up the Stanford application. Mason glanced at the clock on his desk. "Four o'clock and it's almost dark outside. Winter's on its way."

Nola walked over to the tall window. "Snow flurries," she reported. "Maybe we'll have a white Thanksgiving."

Mason stood up, stretching his legs and back, then joined her at the window. "Maybe a white Christmas, too," he murmured, watching the whirl of flakes the size of cotton balls.

"I'm hoping I can stay here for winter break." She leaned

her back against the window. "There's no reason to spend time in Boston."

"Won't your godparents be coming for the holiday?"

She shook her head. "They like Aspen. Or Saint Moritz."

"You could go with them."

"And be ignored? No, thanks." She looked at him out of the corners of her eyes. "You're staying here, too, aren't you?"

Mason shrugged. "That's what happens when you're the new kid on the block. Or the new teacher at Hawkridge, as the case might be." He lifted a quizzical eyebrow. "But you knew that, didn't you?"

Nola's smile was all the more special because of its rarity. "I did. We could have a good time. Drive over to Beech Mountain for skiing, go sledding, all sorts of fun stuff." She placed her palm on his bicep. "Not too many girls stay over. We'd have the place almost to ourselves."

Somehow, the distance between them had diminished until their bodies were barely inches apart. He lifted his hand, hooking a strand of silver-blond hair off her shoulder, rubbing it between his fingertips. Soft, shiny. When he looked up to her face, her skin was smooth and velvety, her lips rosy and plump. As he watched, they parted slightly.

He wanted her, Mason realized. She was only four years younger than he, a pretty, available young girl, and he hadn't had so much as a date—let alone sex—in six months.

A noise in the hallway saved him. When the custodian came in to empty the trash can, Mason was packing up his briefcase. "Hey, Thomas. How's it going? You think this snow will stick?"

"Maybe you could meet in the dining hall, during dinner setup," Nola suggested now as they approached Pink's Cottage. "There are always people going in and out then."

"Good idea." Considering their past, Mason knew he'd do whatever it took to avoid time alone with this woman, even if it meant breaking his own rules.

She stopped at the garden gate. "Thanks for the moral support this afternoon," she said, not quite meeting his eyes. "I'm sure the girls and I will get to know each other better as the days pass."

"I'm sure, too." He wanted to say more, but instead left with a simple—safe—goodbye. As he walked toward home, though, he stopped in his tracks and swore. "Garrett! I forgot to get him from the infirmary."

He jogged back to the Manor and arrived breathless at the school nurse's office ten minutes later. "How's Garrett?" he asked, breathing deeper and faster than he should. Man, was he out of shape.

"Not too bad," Mrs. Ryan said, in her Irish-tinted voice. "He's slept a lot of the day. I'll keep him here with me tomorrow, if you want. Maybe by Wednesday he'll be ready for school."

"Thank you for taking care of him." Mason went through the doorway into the patients' room, where four cots occupied the four corners. Garrett lay listless on the farthest bed, flipping through channels on the television.

"Hey, bud. Ready to go home?"

His son nodded. "Do you still have the car?"

Another thing he'd forgotten—he'd driven to work today because Garrett was too sick to walk. "Sure. I'll go park by the front door and come back to get you."

"Okay."

Mason hurried toward the west door and the faculty parking lot, cursing himself. What kind of father allowed a woman to distract him from the most important person in his life, his own son?

Nola had always wreaked havoc with his brain. He'd spent too much time thinking about her when she was a student, nearly wrecking his career over her. Now…well, now he was just starting to get back on his feet after Gail's death. He wanted to concentrate on Garrett, as he hadn't for the last three miserable years, and rebuild a solid, trusting relationship with his son. A woman in his life—especially *this* woman, for some reason—would complicate his plans for Garrett and their future together as a two-man family. Mason did not want any more complications. He simply couldn't cope.

At least they'd solved the problem of having to spend time together, he and Nola. The arrangement wasn't perfect, but given his reaction whenever he got near her, he thought it the lesser of two evils. He would handle the tutoring alone, in public places, and keep Nola out of his life at the same time. He'd explain to Tommy tomorrow before class.

"There you are. This will save me a phone call."

Mason stopped short at the sight of the headmistress, standing right in front of him. "Jayne. Hi." He could feel bad news waiting to ambush him.

"I talked to Zara," she said, turning to walk with him toward the door. "She's agreed to the tutoring sessions, but she pleaded for one concession."

Zara pleading was hard to imagine. Demand was more her usual style. "And that is…?"

"She doesn't want any of the other girls to know she's in trouble. Because she was cooperating, I agreed she could attend her tutoring lessons at the hunting lodge. Since Nola is a guest, and Pink's Cottage is small, I thought that would work best."

The hunting lodge. Where he lived. Mason fought down his panic. "Jayne, I understand the problem, but meeting Zara at my home would create exactly the situation I've avoided for twelve years."

"But this is different because you'll have Nola there, as well. What kind of questionable behavior could take place when a female teacher is present during all your meetings? You see," she said, smiling as she headed back down the hallway, "you have nothing to worry about."

* * *

MASON'S WAS the last voice Nola expected to hear when she picked up the phone. "We have a problem," he said. "Tommy wants us to meet with Zara at the hunting lodge."

"Why the lodge?"

"It's where Garrett and I live. Zara wants her tutoring kept private, and Tommy didn't want to impose on you."

"Oh." Nola couldn't think of anything else to say. She'd never been invited to Mason's home as a student. She didn't want to be there as an adult, either. Meeting him in a school setting was hard enough—look at how she'd lost her control this afternoon and practically confessed the crush she'd developed the moment she'd first seen him. Would she be able to trust herself in a more intimate environment?

"I don't like the idea," he said over her silence. "But I can't think of any way to get out of it."

"No. I don't suppose there is one." She rubbed her eyes with her fingertips. "We'll just have to deal with Zara and the situation. Graduation is only ten weeks away."

"True." He paused. "And in order to be ready, we need to set up a study program. I'd suggest a meeting somewhere else, but Garrett's still sick. Could you…" Another hesitation. "Could you come by for a little while tonight?"

Nola clenched her free hand. "Of course. What would be a good time?"

They settled the details and ended the call. Then Nola went into the bedroom and threw herself facedown on the bed with both fists clenched in her hair. She didn't know whether to laugh, cry or swear.

So she did some of all three.

OLDER THAN THE Manor by twenty years, the Hawkridge hunting lodge had given Howard Ridgely a place to live while personally supervising the construction of his castle. With admirable foresight, Howard had sited the timber-and-stone lodge more than a mile from the cottages and the main house itself, so the porches on all sides could offer uninterrupted views of the mountains. Nola left her cottage at seven forty-five and arrived precisely at eight o'clock, but only because she walked fast and ignored the scenery.

Mason stepped onto the front porch as she came up the flagstone path. "Welcome. I'm glad to see you didn't get lost."

"I used to wander up this way when I was at Hawkridge." She pointed to a corner of the porch overlooking a rocky streambed. "I sat there sometimes to do my homework." Following the rail around, she nodded at the wider side porch. "I slept out here, on summer nights when I could sneak out."

Mason leaned back against the wall, hands in his pockets. "Thanks for not telling me until now. I would have been obligated to turn you in. How did you get away from the dorm?"

She shrugged. "It's pretty easy, really. The stairwell doors aren't locked because of fire regulations. Sometimes, you put your pillows under the covers, turn your music on and leave the light burning—they peek in and assume you've fallen asleep. That worked with old Miss Ratcliffe. She didn't see well. Otherwise, you wait until after bed check. I wouldn't be surprised, though, if there aren't still a couple of weak links on the dorm staff."

He grinned. "We might have to get you to do a presentation at the next faculty meeting on what the girls know that we don't."

"Breaking Out Is So Very Easy To Do?"

The grin became a chuckle. "Something like that." He led the way back to the front door and ushered her inside. "I hope you don't mind dogs." A scuffling, scratching noise approached from the darkness at the far end of the entry hall.

"Um…" Nola didn't really know whether she minded dogs or not. She'd never had a pet, and rarely visited houses where the animals made an appearance. "Will it bite?"

The scratching, panting sounds got louder, came closer, and then a pack of dogs hurtled into the light, a swirl of bodies brown and gold and white, with wild eyes, dripping tongues and sharp, glistening teeth. Backed up against the door, with her leather bag shielding her chest, Nola held her breath as she was nosed, barked at and jumped on.

The calmest of the four was a plump golden dog with soft brown eyes and white hair on its face. It contented itself with sniffing Nola's hand—a strange but not unpleasant feeling.

"I'm sorry." Mason's face was red as he grabbed the two brown dogs by their collars and dragged them backward, pushing the smallest away with the side of his foot. "They're harmless, but energetic. I didn't realize..." He cleared his throat. "Go into the living room," he said, nodding toward the right, "and I'll put them up."

Nola swallowed and started to breathe again. "Okay."

"Come on, Angel, Gimp. Let's get a treat." The dogs obeyed instantly, following Mason in the direction from which they'd come. Nola wiped the back of her hand on her slacks as she went into the room on the right, frowning when she found her pants damp from being licked. Where was the nearest dry-cleaning shop? Did dog drool stain wool?

She barely had time to appreciate the huge stone fireplace with its flickering log fire, the rich leather chairs and sofas, the bright wool rugs in Native American designs, before the patter of bare feet on wood drew her gaze to the doorway.

Garrett entered with a sideways slide over the polished floor. "Ms. Shannon, I'm so glad you're here! Come see our zoo!"

Mason returned a second later, without the slide. "That's not happening tonight, Garrett. You're sick. We've got work to do." He put his hands on his son's shoulders and headed him toward the hall. "Get back on the couch."

The boy slipped out of his grasp. "Aw, Dad. Wouldn't she

like to see the bunnies? And the lizards?" He looked at Nola again. "There's Rattles the Raccoon and a bunch of turtles plus Homer, and Squeaky the Squirrel. We've got two hamsters, and four gerbils and a million mice, 'cause they just had babies, but most of those'll go to feed the snakes."

Nola flinched. "I'm sure that's fascinating, Garrett. But…"

"Not tonight," Mason insisted. "Get back to the den, son." Garrett opened his mouth to protest, but Mason narrowed his eyes. "Now, please."

Whatever message passed between the two sets of dark brown eyes convinced Garrett to yield. "Okay." His tone conveyed significant disappointment. "'Night, Ms. Shannon." Shoulders slumped, feet dragging, he went back the way he'd come.

"Sorry." Mason pulled out a chair for her at a big round table near the fire. "Sorry about the dogs, and that Garrett pestered you."

"It's okay." When he shook his head, Nola stepped closer. "I just wasn't expecting so many dogs, that's all. And if it weren't so late, I would be glad to have Garrett show me his animals. It sounds like there are quite a few of them." By effort of will, she managed to prevent herself from touching him, keeping her hand at her side, then parking herself in the chair. Close call.

Mason smiled wryly, took the next seat over and opened a legal pad. "He has a talent for finding the injured and needy animals in these mountains, and for treating them. Our local veterinarian will let Garrett nurse some of his less dangerous patients after he's done surgery. Squeaky, for instance, got hit by a car. The vet set his leg, then gave him to Garrett to care for until he can be released."

"Garrett doesn't mind letting them go again?"

"No, because he sees them again in his wanderings." At her incredulous expression, he nodded. "I've been there. We kept a skunk for a while, and a year later, out walking we came upon the little guy. He started to lift his tail, to spray his scent, but Garrett spoke to him and the skunk calmed down. Even came over and took one of the peanuts Garrett carries all the time, then scampered away without making an issue."

"That's amazing."

"Yes, but it's not why you're here."

Nola sighed, and opened her leather binder on the tabletop. "True. We should get some work done. The goal, I gather, is to see that Zara passes algebra and physics so she can graduate. Do you know what her problem is? Are the subjects simply too much for her?"

Mason leaned back in his chair, one arm stretched out to toy with his pen on the legal pad. "Not at all. She's brighter than most of the girls in her class. But she's tricky to handle."

"I noticed." Looking at him splintered her concentration, so Nola focused on her own page of notes. "Has she been a problem before?"

"Not really. Her grade for the first semester was a low B—perfectly acceptable. But for the last grading period, she pulled a D-minus. I meant to talk to her." Jabbing his pen into his pad, Mason blew out a frustrated breath. "I just didn't get to it before spring break."

He looked tired, Nola realized. Not just weary from the day, but long-term exhausted. Without the teasing smile and the force of his personality dominating the conversation, she noticed the shadows under his eyes, the sharpness of his cheekbones and jawline. Though his arm had felt strong when she touched him, the green sweater he wore hung loose on his shoulders.

Nola brought her mind back to the issue at hand. "So what can we do to help her bring up her grades?"

Sitting forward, Mason braced his elbows on the table. "I've been thinking about what Gail would have done. She taught biology, but her real talent was her ability to connect with the girls, change their attitudes."

"That's a valuable asset."

He smiled, a mixture of regret and pride. "Gail was great. I think she would use the first few tutoring sessions as a means of gaining Zara's confidence, encouraging her to share her feelings. She would help Zara deal with what's going on while improving her command of the material."

Nola nodded. "Do you think you can do that?"

Eyebrows raised, he stared at her. "Not *me*."

Her internal alarm bell rang. "Mason…"

"It's bad enough I'm bringing her into my home. I've never done that with another student. I try to keep my private life just that. Private."

"I remember." She flattened her hand on top of her page of notes. "I didn't even know you were getting married until I saw the announcement of your wedding in the alumnae newsletter." As soon as she said it, she knew she'd made a mistake.

His gaze sharpened, fixed on her face. "You sound… peeved about that."

At least he hadn't used the word *jealous*. Nola relaxed her hand and gave a small shrug. "I graduated, you moved on to new students. I understand the reasons now. At the time, I thought we were better friends than that." Would he believe the lie?

He accepted it, whether he believed her or not. "Which is why *you* need to be the one to deal with Zara's feelings. You're a woman. She can share them with you safely."

The alarm bell had become a siren. "I don't think—"

Before she could finish, Mason covered the back of her hand with his own. His thumb slipped underneath to press against her palm, a contact that sent bursts of energy spitting along her nerves.

Holding her gaze with his own, he said, "Jayne has asked you to help Zara not only because of your expertise in math, but because the girl desperately needs someone to care about. You have the background, the experience and the empathy to understand what she feels.

"What you have to do, Nola, is become Zara's friend."

"That's impossible," she said hoarsely. "I can't."

Chapter Six

Mason watched the expressions race through Nola's blue eyes—worry, anger, and most of all, fear.

"What is it?" He gripped her hand tighter. "Why can't you become Zara's friend?"

She stared at him, and he felt the tension in her body vibrate through his own. Or maybe that was simply the contact of her skin against his, driving his pulse to a pounding beat.

"Nola?"

She drew a deep, shuddering breath, and jerked her hand away. Her clenched fist came to rest between her breasts.

"Nothing…" she said finally. Her gaze wandered the room, never settling in one place more than a moment. "Nothing's wrong. Of course that's what we need to do." She shook her head as she closed her notebook. "I'm not sure how well this will work, though, since I turned her in to Jayne for smoking. But I'll do what I can."

She'd given him far less than the whole truth, and Mason was tempted to push the issue. But he forced himself to think of the job rather than the woman. "Okay. We'll meet here with Zara next Monday afternoon at three-thirty. Together, we'll explain the situation and what we propose to do. After a while,

I'll leave you alone with her and the two of you can start building a rapport."

"Theoretically," Nola inserted. "I hope there's a plan B somewhere."

"We won't need a plan B. You'll find some common ground and hit it off. Then we'll start making progress."

"If you say so." She sounded anything but certain. And she didn't look at him as she stood, preparing to leave. Instead, she studied the drawings hanging on the walls.

"Airplane plans," she said finally. "Are you still designing planes?"

He dug his hands into the pockets of his slacks. "Not the past several years. Before Gail…got sick…I did some good work."

Now she did look at him. "Can I ask what was wrong?"

He tried to relax his hands, his arms, before he ripped the seams of his pockets. "Primary pulmonary hypertension. Her lungs failed, they don't know why. She was a candidate for a transplant."

"I don't know anything about that disease. I'm sorry."

"Thanks." He walked to the fireplace, kicked at a half-burned log that had fallen forward on the grate. "She was simply tired at first, and she had a hard time catching her breath on the walk home from the school. Some coughing, now and then. By the time the doctors figured out what was wrong, she was seriously sick."

"That must have been hard. For all three of you."

"And her parents. They live near Asheville on a farm. Garrett visits as often as he can." He managed a rueful laugh. "And they're here about as much as I can stand. Losing Gail has made Garrett that much more precious to them."

She accepted the change of subject without protest. "I'm sure he enjoys himself. There are probably lots of animals to care for."

Mason followed as Nola walked to the front door. "Dogs and

cats, chickens, goats, horses, cows and sheep. They also have a pair of donkeys and a few alpacas hanging around for fun."

"I can't imagine taking care of so many creatures." She opened the door and stepped out into the chilly spring night. "But then, I'm the only creature I've ever been responsible for."

"Many people would envy you that freedom." He stood just behind her, close enough to breathe in her intriguing scent, to see, even in the darkness, the individual wisps of silvery hair clinging to the nape of her neck. His body warmed, quickened, in response.

"Freedom isn't quite—isn't always—the blessing it's advertised to be." Her slender shoulders lifted as she drew a deep breath, and the sound alone aroused him even more. "The grass is always greener…"

Without thinking—or thinking about stopping—Mason rested his hands lightly on those shoulders, his fingertips brushing her collarbones. The step he took brought his body against hers.

"There are advantages to relationships," he murmured against her temple. "Nobody likes being alone all the time." Her cheek was smooth against his lips. He shifted his hold, started to turn her into his arms.

And found himself holding nothing at all. Nola had bolted down the steps to the ground. Backing away, she said, "I-I'll see you tomorrow. I hope Garrett keeps feeling better. Good night."

"Nola—"

But she whirled and vanished into the spring darkness, leaving Mason alone on the porch, cursing himself as a damn fool for the second time that day.

NOLA KEPT TO HERSELF for the rest of the week, eating lunch in her classroom, working hard on grading and lesson preparation in the evenings, avoiding Mason at all costs. A rainy weekend contributed to her isolation. On Saturday morning she called Ted and hung up reassured by his steady, temperate response to her description of her work. His kind of calm was what she wanted in her life. What she needed.

Not tempestuous teenagers and handsome, lonesome widowers.

During lunch break on her second Monday of classes, she'd finished her sandwich but was still at work grading quizzes when Alice Tolbert stuck her head through the partially closed door. "Woman, what are you doing, eating at your desk? You need to come join the rest of us in the teachers' lounge, get out of your classroom for a little while." She flipped one long nail across the edges of the papers Nola had yet to tackle. "You're making too much work for yourself, here. Let the girls check their own homework."

"I will," Nola promised. "But since I haven't been with them all year, I want to get an idea of where each of them is first." And she wanted to avoid any chance of running into Mason Reed.

Alice sat on the nearest student table. "Well, okay. As long as I know you aren't avoiding us."

Nola tried not to wince as she looked Alice in the eye.

"I wanted to let you know," the English teacher continued, "that faculty volleyball starts this afternoon. We play twice a week for a couple of hours. We usually have a student audience rooting for both sides, and a good time is had by all. We'll expect to see you—" She stopped when Nola shook her head. "You can't play?"

"I… No. I'm not much into sports."

"Well, come cheer for us, then. It's just for fun."

"I'm not sure I've got the time. I'm still working on my research, you know, even while I'm teaching here. And Jayne has asked me to tutor a couple of students."

Alice put her weight on both feet, straightening her back

and squaring her shoulders. "I understand." The lift of her chin and the cool expression in her dark eyes showed exactly how insulted she felt. "I won't pester you any longer."

"You aren't—" But she spoke to empty air, because Alice had already slipped out the door. The bell ending lunch period rang as Nola sat berating herself for having offended not only Alice but probably—once the story made the rounds—the entire faculty.

Three one-sided math classes later, the school day ended. Nola erased her board, straightened her desk and packed her briefcase. With no other excuses to dawdle, she flipped off the classroom lights and started walking toward the lodge.

A light wind stirred the cool mountain air and the new leaves uncurling behind the fading dogwood flowers. Puffy white clouds drifted across the brilliant blue sky, and daffodils danced at the edge of the forest.

Nola's mood did not, however, match the afternoon. She'd been sleeping badly, waking over and over again to think about those minutes on the porch with Mason. Had he really intended to kiss her? Or had she imagined it?

Why couldn't she get her mind—her heart, her body, whatever was causing the problem—off this one-way track?

Barking dogs answered her knock on the lodge's front door, so she sat in a rocking chair to wait for Mason and Garrett. And Zara, of course, the girl she was supposed to make friends with. She'd made few friends in her life, however, except Ted. Oh, and Mason Reed. But he had married someone else.

Now, though, he wasn't married. If he was interested and she was interested, and they were both adults...

Her chest tightened at the thought and her palms grew damp. She didn't want Mason, didn't *need* Mason in her life. And he didn't need her. Nola remembered Gail Chance, though she'd never taken one of her classes—she'd been a warm, loving woman with a talent for connecting with her students. A terrific mother, too, no doubt—patient, warm, funny and involved.

Everything, in fact, that Nola was not. Ted would be the caretaker in their family—he'd grown up with several siblings and he understood the dynamics between parents and children. He knew Nola well enough to understand her limitations and still he wanted a relationship. So he wouldn't ask more than she could supply.

Mason, on the other hand, would expect…everything. And Nola simply didn't have it to give.

When the silver SUV pulled into the driveway, Garrett's door opened first. He climbed out on his own, but without the energy Nola would have expected. Mason slid out of the driver's seat, and Zara came around from the other side of the car, a scowl on her face and a slump to her shoulders.

Nola sighed to herself. This was going to be impossible.

Garrett walked up the steps. "Hi, Ms. Shannon."

"Hi, Garrett. How was school today?"

He shrugged. "Okay."

Mason came up behind him. "Hi." No smile, no glint in his eye. "Tommy had to hunt Zara down. I'm sorry to keep you waiting."

"No problem. I've enjoyed just sitting here."

He opened the front door. "You might want to stay seated until the dogs get outside. They're pretty wild after being inside all day."

The animals rushed out, and Nola saw that "wild" was something of an understatement. But with Garrett, Mason and Zara all giving them attention, the younger dogs left her alone. Only the golden dog—Angel, Mason had called her—came over to say hello. She nosed at Nola's hand, and seemed to smile when Nola ran her fingers lightly over the soft fur on her head. Then Angel saw that her friends had left the porch with Garrett. After bestowing a final lick on the back of Nola's hand, she followed them into the trees.

"You're safe," Mason said to Nola. "Come on inside."

Zara snorted. "She's afraid of those dogs?" She rolled her eyes. "Man, what a wimp."

Mason stopped in the process of pulling a third chair to the table they'd worked at last week. "Insults will not be tolerated, Zara." Once again, Nola was amazed by the edge that soft drawl could acquire. "Be respectful, or you're going to find yourself in serious trouble."

The girl dropped into the chair he'd provided. "Whatever." Arms crossed, she let her head fall back and stared at the ceiling. Mason motioned for Nola to take a seat, then sat down in the chair on Zara's other side.

"Here's the deal," he told the girl. "You're failing physics and algebra. If you want to graduate, you have to pass these courses. Ms. Shannon and I are here to help you do that. Is there a problem with this plan?"

Zara didn't move. "It's stupid."

Mason folded his arms on the table. "Why?"

"I'm just going to get some stupid job. I don't need physics or algebra to do that."

"That's all you want out of life? A stupid job?"

The girl shrugged. "I gotta earn money to live on."

"You could earn money doing something you liked." He glanced at Nola, inviting her to join the conversation.

She wasn't sure what she could contribute that he hadn't already said, and told him so with a shrug.

He frowned at her, then turned back to Zara. "If you could be paid for doing what you love, what would you choose?"

Zara threw a nasty grin in Nola's direction. "Do they pay people to smoke cigarettes?"

Nola felt as if a high-tension wire had snapped inside her brain. "Only if they're researching lung cancer," she retorted.

"I should know. My father died of lung cancer at the ripe old age of thirty-eight." She looked down at her hands, gripped together in her lap, and then at Zara again. "I was six years old."

Zara jerked upright to stare back with her jaw hanging loose. Mason was startled, as well. He hadn't remembered that detail of Nola's life.

After a moment's silence, he cleared his throat. "Try again," he told Zara. "What do you like to do?"

After a long pause, she said, "I draw."

"Okay, what kind of drawing?"

"Cartoons," she admitted in a voice barely above a whisper.

Before Mason could comment, Nola leaned forward. "What if you could earn money drawing cartoons?"

"I still wouldn't need physics or algebra." Zara didn't stay knocked down for long.

"But a high-school diploma comes in handy," Mason pointed out, "for jobs at newspapers and magazines."

"To hell with that." Zara snorted. "I'll publish my stuff on the Internet, and everybody will come looking for me when they see how good it is."

"Perhaps." Nola nodded. "How will you afford a computer? The one you're using stays here when you leave, I believe."

Zara shrugged a shoulder. "I can work at a restaurant. In a gas station."

"Do you know what the minimum wage is these days?"

"The what?"

"How much you'll get paid by the hour in a job like that," Mason explained.

"Less than seven dollars," Nola put in before Zara spoke. "If you work ten hours a day, six days a week, at that job, how much will you make in a month?"

The girl stared at her. "How the hell should I know?"

Nola scooted her chair around until she and Zara could look at a piece of paper side by side. "This is how you figure that out."

Mason sat back as she explained the calculation. Within ten minutes, he knew the two of them had forgotten his presence. Smiling, he left them alone together.

When he returned at four-thirty, Nola and Zara were just finishing up. "I wouldn't earn enough money to live on," the girl told him. "I'd have to work two jobs."

"Lots of people do." He grinned at Nola but found her avoiding his eyes, so he returned his gaze to Zara. "Remember—tomorrow, same time and place. We'll work on the physics homework for this week."

"Man, that sucks." Shaking her head, Zara picked up her backpack just as Garrett stepped into the room. "Hey, buddy. Found any new turtles lately?"

"A big box turtle. I named him Homer."

"Cool. Got time to show him to me?"

"Sure!" He grabbed her by the arm. "It's time to feed the snakes, too. Want to help?"

"I wouldn't miss it." Heedless of the adults staring at them in amazement, the two of them headed toward the sunroom which served as an animal hospital.

Mason waited until he heard that door shut. Then he turned to Nola. "First, I want to say I'm sorry about your father."

She was gathering the papers she and Zara had been working with and didn't look at him. "Thank you."

"I can't recall, off the top of my head—when did you lose your mother?"

Without answering, she pulled a file folder out of her briefcase, slipped the pages into it, then wrote a label on the tab.

He went to stand beside the table. "Nola?"

Still avoiding his eyes, she blew out a breath. "My mother committed suicide a year after my father died. Said she couldn't live without him." She shrugged one shoulder. "I wasn't enough to stay around for."

Horror blanked his mind for a moment. Then he thought of Gail's regret at missing out on Garrett's life. "She must have been severely depressed, Nola. Not thinking straight. You know she didn't really mean that."

Nola looked at him, then, with such stark despair in her eyes that he almost wished she hadn't. "The logic of her action is inescapable." She blinked, and the despair vanished. "But it was a long time ago, and I don't think about either of them very often. Zara's comment hit a nerve, that's all. Don't look so worried."

He couldn't let it go that easily. "Did you grow up with relatives?" Before she could answer, he remembered. "No. That, I do remember—you were the last of the family. And your guardians rarely showed up."

One shoulder lifted in a shrug. "I saw them every few months. They'd fly in for a week or so, then fly out again. There was a long string of nannies. I couldn't blame anyone for avoiding me—I was a difficult child." She gave him a wry smile. "As an adult, I try to be easier to get along with. Thank you for helping me learn how to cooperate."

"No problem." Until now, anyway, when he couldn't seem to get her off his mind. "Nola, about last week. I was—"

She held up a hand to stop him. "You don't have to apologize. It doesn't matter."

"Doesn't matter?" He clenched his jaw.

"I mean, nothing happened. I misunderstood, that's all, and—and panicked."

"About what?" He took a step forward, so he was standing directly beside her.

Nola sidestepped farther around the table. "I thought you might try to kiss me."

"And that doesn't matter?"

"No. I mean…" She dragged her fingers through her hair.

"I mean, I was wrong. That's all. You wouldn't." Her eyes widened. "Would you?"

He owed her the truth, though he could barely admit it to himself. "Yes."

"Oh." After a pause, she said, "But now you're sorry?"

"I… Yes."

Her face changed, and her hand dropped to her side. "Don't worry about that, either. Apology accepted." She collected more papers, sliding them into her briefcase.

Mason felt everything except relief. "That's all you're going to say?"

She shrugged one shoulder. "We don't have to make an issue out of this. You experienced a momentary lapse in judgment. You've apologized and I've accepted the apology. I should thank you for avoiding an unpleasant situation between us."

"Unpleasant? Situation?"

"Yes." She drew a deep breath. "I made the mistake of admitting I had a crush on you when I was a student. It's understandable that you might want to discover if that attraction still exists. Fortunately, I've grown up, and you thought the better of your impulse. Now we move on." Briefcase in hand, she walked to the front door. "Tell Garrett I said goodbye."

Left alone, Mason wondered if he'd been picked up by a tornado and deposited in a different dimension. He'd somehow been transformed from the wise, levelheaded mentor into a lust-driven adolescent rebuffed by a more experienced woman. He didn't like the change. Nola Shannon couldn't dismiss him so easily.

Even more important, he wouldn't allow her to belittle herself so completely.

MASON ANSWERED the phone a couple of hours later to hear Ruth Ann Blakely on the line. "Is Zara Kauffman still working with you?"

"She left here about four-thirty. She's not at dinner?"

"Nope. She isn't in her room, either, and the senior hall monitor—Mrs. Bixby—is having palpitations. Again."

Mason wasn't surprised, especially after Nola's confession about the ease with which the girls could disappear from the dorm.

"Damn Zara, anyway." Ruth Ann gave a frustrated sigh. "How many times has she gone missing this year? Six? Ten? Why does she keep sneaking off? Couldn't she stick to the rules for a few more weeks?"

He dragged a hand through his hair. "I thought she was feeling fairly cooperative when she left this afternoon. She and Nola seemed to get along. Maybe Zara ended up at Pink's Cottage."

"I'll call Nola," Ruth Ann said. "Listen, are you playing volleyball this year? We're short on both sides. Nola declined, and she really ticked Alice off. Anyway, you're a good man to have on the serving line. Come play for my team Wednesday afternoon."

"I can't." The words were out before he'd even come up with a reason.

"Are you sure?"

Fortunately, the reasons came to mind quickly. "I'm afraid so, although I appreciate the invitation. But I'm working with Zara Wednesday at three-thirty."

"Assuming we find her?"

"Right. And Garrett's still not a hundred percent."

"How about next week?"

He didn't want to say no outright. "Let me get through this week, first."

"All right. But I'm not giving up. Count on a phone call from me Sunday night."

"I'll look forward to it."

As he hung up, Garrett came into the kitchen. "Who was it?"

"Ms. Blakely, looking for Zara. You wouldn't happen to know where she went, do you?"

Garrett shook his head. "She headed down through the trees in back, like she usually does."

"She's been here before?"

"She helped me bring Rattles home, remember? And a couple of the turtles. I run into her sometimes, out in the woods. She's got a cave out there, where she goes to smoke." He clapped a hand over his mouth and looked at Mason in dismay. "I wasn't supposed to say that."

Mason ruffled his son's hair. "I knew about the smoking. I didn't know you spent time with her."

"She's okay." Garrett shrugged a shoulder. "What's for dinner?"

"Good question." Mason turned to the pantry, willing to forget about women in the search for sustenance. "Is this our night for a box or a can?"

Chapter Seven

This time, when Garrett woke up at 2:00 a.m. and checked on his dad, the big bed was empty. He stood for a minute in the doorway, remembering how, when he was a real little kid, he'd show up in the middle of the night and his mom would wave her arm for him to come around to her side of the bed so he could crawl in between her and his dad. He remembered how warm he'd felt. How safe, between their two big bodies. Nothing in the world could hurt him there.

Squinting against the burn of tears in his eyes, Garrett turned and padded down the hall to the stairs. Maybe his dad had decided he was hungry. The box of macaroni and cheese and the frozen peas they'd fixed for dinner hadn't kept Garrett full, so he'd made himself a bowl of ice cream before he went to bed. His dad had poured a glass of wine, but that had been his only dessert.

The kitchen was dark, except for the night-light they left burning by the sink. Mom had bought it on one of their trips to the beach—a pretty scallop shell that glowed soft pink when the light was on. But his dad wasn't sitting at the table eating, or watching TV in the family room.

Garrett finally caught sight of him from one of the living-room windows. He was sitting in one of the rocking chairs on the side porch, staring out into the dark. He had to be cold out there, with only sweatpants and a T-shirt on. Angel lay with her head on his ankles, so at least his feet were warm. The rocking chair slowly moved back and forth, so he wasn't asleep. What could he be thinking about, out there this late?

After a while, Garrett gave up watching. He got a drink from the kitchen, then climbed the stairs and headed back to his room.

At the doorway of his parents' room, he stopped again. Maybe...

On his dad's side of the bed, he turned off the lamp. Then he went around to his mom's side, pulled the covers out from underneath her pillow and climbed in.

Maybe, if he stayed real still and listened carefully, he could hear what she wanted him to do. There had to be some way to make his dad try again. Garrett hadn't gotten any great ideas since he'd asked for help, at the pond with Homer. But being in her bed with his head on her pillow might help. She could whisper, and he felt certain he'd understand what he had to do.

"Help me, Mom. Before it's too late."

He wasn't sure how he would know when it was too late or what would happen. He just knew he was running out of time.

Tuesday morning, Nola arrived in the dining hall as breakfast was being served. She found Ruth Ann seated at the Third West table.

"Did Zara turn up last night?"

Ruth Ann nodded and waved at the chair beside her. "Have a seat. Yes, when I checked at lights-out, there she was, innocently stretched out on her bed with a physics book."

"Did she say why she missed dinner?"

"She wasn't hungry," Ruth Ann said with a skeptical glance over the rim of her coffee mug. "She went for a walk in the woods instead."

Nola nodded at the server who offered to pour coffee for her. "Thank you." Then she looked at Ruth Ann. "That could be true."

"Oh, I suppose." Ruth Ann leaned her elbows on the table and propped her chin on her hands. "I only wish she could understand that we don't want to be jailers—we want to be sure she's safe. Not everyone is out to punish her."

"Teenagers have to feel persecuted, don't they? It's part of the separation process." If they had someone to separate from, anyway.

"Exactly. Zara just takes it to extremes." She sighed. "Meanwhile, between noon and 6:00 p.m. yesterday, somebody keyed all the school vans and cars."

Nola frowned. "Keyed? I don't understand."

"They scraped a sharp metal object, like a key, down the side of each vehicle from headlamps to brake lights."

"The same person who broke the windows over spring break? Do the police think the vandal is a student here?"

Ruth Ann shrugged. "It seems likely, but how can we tell unless someone confesses?" She stirred sugar into her coffee. "On a brighter note, I have a project I want your help on."

"What is it?" Nola spooned up a mouthful of sugared oatmeal.

"I want to wake the sleeping prince. Snow White with a gender twist."

Nola put the spoon down untouched. "I beg your pardon?"

"Mason," Ruth Ann said. "Mason Reed. I want to shake him up and bring him back to life. Surely you remember how he was when he first came to Hawkridge. Energetic and devilish and…and alive."

Nola didn't want to admit just how much she did remember.

"But since he lost Gail," Ruth Ann continued, "all that energy has vanished."

Nola forced her brain to work. "Well, he's sad. In mourning. He loved her." A hard thing to say aloud for the first time.

"Yes. We all loved Gail—she was a sweetheart. But

Mason's a young man. I want to nudge him back to the land of the living."

"You don't need my help for that."

"Yes, I do. He's practically been a recluse these past three years, and he's getting worse. But since you're helping him tutor Zara you'll be seeing him frequently."

"Strictly for work."

Ruth Ann waved away the objection. "Still, you're there, and you can draw him out. Now, the first thing I think we need to do is get him to play volleyball."

"I'm not—"

"I know you told Alice you have to work. But for Mason you can change your mind, right? Just move the tutoring session to, say, five o'clock. That gives you time for volleyball first. Maybe Zara will even come watch, which would be good for her, too. It's been nearly impossible to involve her in activities with the other girls. She's a loner, if ever there was one."

Nola could sympathize, but… "I really don't think—"

"The other big issue is the spring dance." Ruth Ann downed the last of her coffee. "I'm chairing the committee this year. We need students and teachers to work on various aspects of the dance. I want you and Mason to help out."

"I can't volunteer Mason for anything. And I don't—"

"Oh, come on. It'll be fun." Ruth Ann crumpled her napkin into her cereal bowl and got to her feet. "Maybe you could handle decorations and Mason could work on the music. Or vice versa."

Nola picked up her tray and followed her to the trash cans. "I have never successfully chosen pillows that matched a couch, let alone decorated a ballroom."

"Fine, though it's the kids who come up with the ideas and do the work. You just supervise. We'll let Mason do the decorations, then, and you can handle the music. That's even easier. We always hire a deejay." Before Nola could protest further,

Ruth Ann lifted a hand and swerved toward the exit. "I've got a group lesson at eight. I'll call you about the dance. Thanks!"

Leaving her tray on the conveyor belt to the kitchen, Nola walked back through the dining hall. She didn't miss the whispers of girls as she went by, or the avoidance techniques practiced by faculty members as they chatted over a final cup of coffee before the day began. Mason and Ruth Ann appeared to be her only allies.

And she wasn't sure about Mason. She hadn't given him a chance to explain about the kiss. Her concentration was fractured already, having him just down the hall. Thinking he might want her... No. She couldn't go there.

Nola pushed through the doors into the science-and-math hallway, glanced toward her classroom and gasped. As if her thoughts had conjured him up, Mason stood by her door.

"Good morning." He looked at her with concern. "Are you okay?"

"Um, yes. Of course. I just didn't expect anyone to be standing there."

"Sorry. But I needed to talk to you before classes start. About Zara."

She stepped by him, careful not to brush against his arm, and flipped on the lights in her room. "What about Zara?"

"Well, actually about Garrett and Zara. Garrett's fever is back this morning and he's coughing. The first doctor's appointment I could get today was for four o'clock. So I'm going to have to turn the physics tutoring session over to you this afternoon."

"Oh." She could hardly complain, when his son was sick. "I'm sorry he's gotten worse."

"Thanks. Since Gail... Well, I'd rather be safe than sorry. Anyway, I'm sure you can manage to explain electricity to Zara. I brought you a textbook, just in case."

"I remember the basics. V equals IR, right?"

"You got it. And I'll tell Zara to meet you at Pink's Cottage instead of the lodge."

"Oh." She hadn't thought that far. "She could come to my classroom…"

Mason shook his head. "Remember, we're incognito, more or less. And maybe you can get her to open up a little, even tell you where she went during dinner last night."

"I can try." She didn't want to burden him with her doubts. "Don't worry about us—we'll manage this afternoon. Just make sure Garrett's taken care of. And…" She took a deep breath. "And let me know how he is, please?"

"I will." He lifted a hand, and for a second she thought he was going to touch her face with his fingertips. But the warning bell rang at that moment and three girls came through the door. Mason dropped his hand, nodded and left quickly, though not without receiving greetings and giggles from the girls in the room and several outside in the hallway.

As Nola had suspected, every student at Hawkridge still developed a crush on Mason Reed. She hoped they didn't take the experience as seriously as she had.

And she prayed her own simple crush wasn't developing into something infinitely more complicated. Like love.

ZARA RANG the doorbell at three forty-five.

"You're late," Nola commented after her "hello, come in" got no response.

"Had a meeting." Zara gestured around the room. "Sure is a lot of pink in here."

Nola was determined to maintain a positive attitude, if it killed her. "I have to wonder about old Josiah. Do you think he left it this way?"

The girl eyed the crocheted doilies, the frilly white curtains, the pale pink roses on the dark pink carpet. "Queer as a three-dollar bill, if he did," she said.

"Have you ever, in your entire life, been polite to anyone?" Exasperated, Nola glared at her guest.

Zara grinned. "Nah."

Nola rolled her eyes. "I'll get some soda and chips. Have a seat at the dining-room table. There's a nice thick pad, so we won't hurt the wood."

"I'm *so* glad." Zara dropped into a chair, heard it creak and got up fast. "Maybe I need something sturdier."

Returning with the snacks, Nola shrugged. "Maybe you need to sit, instead of flop."

In a second, Zara had shouldered her backpack and stalked to the door. "I don't have to take insults. I'm out of here."

"You can dish them out," Nola said, "but you can't take them?"

Hand on the doorknob, the girl hesitated.

Nola took advantage of the opportunity. "I'll be glad to tell Ms. Thomas that you chose to end the tutoring sessions, and will be failing math and physics. She could probably send you home now, instead of waiting until the end of the semester."

Zara heaved a sigh and turned around. Back at the table, she made a show out of gently lowering herself into the antique chair. Then she looked at Nola. "Better?"

"It didn't creak this time." She didn't give in to the urge to smile—Zara didn't deserve such positive reinforcement. Yet. "Mr. Reed said we should review electricity theory. What can you tell me about electrons?"

With a huge sigh, Zara answered the question. She appeared to understand the concepts, so Nola moved quickly into the math problems associated with the material. They continued working, concentrating fiercely, until she felt her back muscles cramp from staying in one position for too long. A glance at her watch as she straightened up made her gasp.

"I don't believe it!" She showed Zara the dial.

"It's after seven?" The girl slapped her pencil down on the page. "I missed dinner."

"Again," Nola said, nodding. "At least today you have a good excuse—and a witness."

Zara rolled her eyes. "That's great, except I'll starve till breakfast."

After a moment of hesitation, Nola took the risk. "I can do something about that. Finish up the problem while I get dinner together."

Zara hesitated, too. Then she shrugged and went back to work.

Nola held her sigh of relief until she reached the kitchen. There, she put one of Mrs. Werner's casseroles in the microwave to warm and tossed together a green salad. The small kitchen table was just the right size for two people, though she'd never imagined she'd be sharing it with Zara. If she'd expected anyone to sit in the other chair, it might have been Mason.

Maybe he'd be pleased to know she and Zara had eaten together. He wanted her to become the girl's friend, and this was a perfect opportunity. She couldn't demand Zara's confidence, though, just because she'd made dinner. How did one engineer a relationship?

She called Zara into the kitchen and stood behind her own chair as the teenager entered. "Have a seat," she said with a gesture at the other place.

But Zara surveyed the kitchen first. "More pink."

Nola chuckled. "They took the theme to extremes, didn't they?"

"Yeah. I checked out the bathroom, too. Pink tile." Zara sat down and unfolded the napkin at her place. "I suppose these came with the cottage." She flapped the square of pink linen. "Are the sheets pink, too?"

"White, thank goodness. I don't know if I could fall asleep on pink sheets."

"Black's good. Kinda like you're in a cave all by yourself."
She eyed the casserole as Nola set it on the table. "That looks
like Mrs. W's lasagna."

"It is. Don't you like it?"

"Are you kidding? The best thing about this place is the
food." Without waiting to be served or even invited, Zara
grabbed the serving spoon and ladled lasagna onto her plate.

For the first few minutes, silence reigned as Zara chewed
and Nola tried to think of something to build a conversation
on. She didn't know what high-school seniors—or college
seniors, for that matter—thought about these days. Her only
interest had been mathematics for so many years now, she
couldn't say she thought about much else. And Zara probably
did not want to talk about math.

Halfway through her second helping, Zara looked up. "So,
you're, like, a math genius, right?"

Nola nodded. "Pretty much, though it's uncomfortable to
admit."

The girl shrugged. "Some people are gorgeous, that's the way
they are and they know it. Were your parents geniuses, too?"

"Not that I know of."

"And were you doing algebra when you were three or
something?"

"Nothing so precocious. I didn't know I had a talent for
mathematics until I came to Hawkridge. Mas— Mr. Reed
realized I was different."

"How'd you end up here, anyway? I mean, this is like the
last stop before reform school. Or jail."

Nola took a second helping of her own. "I'd been kicked
out of four other schools."

"Man, that's impressive! What for?"

"Cheating. Smoking." She saw the surprise on Zara's face.
"Oh, yes. Being drunk at school. Disrupting class, refusing to
submit to discipline. Hawkridge was my guardians' last resort."

"You had a guardian?"

"My godparents were my guardians, but they lived mostly in Europe. A committee of bankers and lawyers ran my trust fund."

"So your mom died, too."

"Um, yes."

"You fit right in at Hawkridge, huh?"

"I did."

"And now you're a teacher. That's kinda weird, I guess."

"Very weird. I don't feel older than the rest of you, but I'm supposed to enforce the rules and keep the students in line." For the first time, Zara met Nola's gaze straight on. "And nobody's made that easy."

Nola shook her head slowly. "No, they haven't."

Zara took another forkful of lasagna. "Well, you're pretty hard to warm up to. It'll take a while."

Nola gasped, and then tried to laugh. "Thanks for being honest with me."

"Did you think you were warm and fuzzy?"

"No, but…"

"And you don't have Mr. Reed's advantage."

"What's that?"

"Being male. And hot, for such an old guy." She chewed for a minute. "What year did you graduate?"

"Nineteen ninety-six."

"Right. So you would have been here when Mr. Reed first came."

"Yes."

Zara leaned her elbows on the table. "What was he like when he was twenty-two? Just totally gorgeous?"

Nola hesitated, then said crisply, "He was really good-looking and an excellent teacher. He helped me recognize my talents and gave me a future in the process." She pushed back her chair, got to her feet and picked up her plate. "If you're finished, you can bring your plate to the sink. I rinse each piece before I put it in the dishwasher."

Still seated, the teenager stared at her, mouth open. "What's with the attitude? All I wanted to know was—"

"Could you bring the glasses and the salad bowl, too?" Nola turned her back to the table and busied herself at the sink. After a few seconds Zara clanked her plate and glass on the counter, then returned with the serving dishes. She stood beside Nola for a minute, as if trying to decide what to say. From the corner of her eye, Nola saw her shrug.

"I'm out of here." Zara thumped the swinging door into the dining room with the heel of her hand and stomped through. Papers crackled, then the front door slammed, and the house was quiet once more.

Nola turned off the water and stood motionless, her hands dripping into the sink. Sharing gossip about Mason would probably have created a rapport with Zara, but at what cost? She couldn't believe the girl would have respected her as a teacher if they'd giggled together over a shared crush.

And Zara might be a loner, but Nola wouldn't trust her to keep such juicy gossip to herself. By morning, every student in the school would know that Mr. Reed and Ms. Shannon had had a "thing" when she was a student. She wasn't sure who would be more embarrassed by that development, Mason or herself.

If establishing a relationship with Zara required exposing her most intimate fantasies, her private dreams, then Nola would settle for failure—which was why she'd doubted the success of this enterprise in the first place. She understood relationships between numbers, not people. She'd failed to connect with Zara, pushing her away rather than building the friendship Mason had hoped for.

As a result, she realized, she'd also failed Mason himself.

* * *

ON THURSDAY, Mason forded the lunchtime flow in the main hall of the Manor, entered the administrative offices and got a nod from Jayne Thomas's assistant.

"Go on in."

"Thanks."

The headmistress looked up from her paperwork as he stepped through the doorway. "Good afternoon. How's Garrett feeling?"

"Better." Mason closed the door behind him, then sat in the armchair near the desk. "Still coughing. But the fever's gone."

Jayne nodded. "I can imagine how this worries you. We've had several cases of this flu strain in the school—the girls seemed better, then got hit with a second round of fever and cough. But now they're all improving, thank goodness, and going back to class."

The tension inside him eased a fraction. "I'm glad to hear it."

"Are the tutoring sessions with Zara working out?"

So much for relaxing. "Monday I thought things went well. Tuesday I took Garrett to the doctor, but Nola seemed to feel confident she could handle things. Yesterday…" Was there a way to make this sound better than it was?

"Yes?"

No. "Yesterday was a nightmare. Zara spent the entire two hours sulking, making rude comments and generally obstructing any effort I made to deal with the material. Nola…" Mason shook his head. "Nola contributed almost nothing to the session. I had to ask her a direct question to get any kind of participation at all. Frankly, I was glad to see both of them leave the house."

Jayne frowned. "It sounds like they had some kind of disagreement on Tuesday."

"Over electricity?"

"Maybe Zara refused to cooperate with Nola."

"Could be." He didn't want to voice the other possibility—that Nola had found herself unable to reach out to Zara. Yesterday afternoon he'd been too frustrated to ask.

The headmistress made a note on a legal pad. "I'll talk to Nola and see if I can help in some way. What we can't do is abandon the effort. I really want Zara to graduate, not simply leave."

"I agree."

"Good." She gave him a moment's break and then said, "What else did *you* want to talk about?"

Mason shifted in his chair. "I wanted to let you know that I've been putting out some feelers over the last few months with other schools and businesses. Exploring options, really. Now I'm starting to get responses, requests for interviews. I intend to accept a few of those."

"You're thinking about leaving Hawkridge?" She looked interested, but not furious. "Why?"

He hesitated, framing the reasons. "I think I need a change. I've been doing the same thing for twelve years now, and I feel like I'm operating by remote control. The girls deserve more than I'm giving."

Jayne held up a hand. "You're a fine teacher, Mason. I would have said something if I thought you were doing less than I expected."

"I'm glad you think so. But the heart's gone out of it for me. Maybe I need to teach boys for a while. Maybe I should move into administration, or dig ditches or pick up garbage." He grinned. "I'm considering those options. But staying here, in the same house where Gail was sick, where she died…" He rubbed his fingers over his eyes. "I need something new. Garrett and I both do."

"I don't suppose offering you more money would make a difference."

Mason shook his head. "Money's not the issue." Since his ancestors' arrival on the Carolina coast in the seventeenth century, the Reeds had always managed to safeguard the family fortune.

To his surprise, the headmistress left her chair and came to stand behind him with her hands on his shoulders, squeezing gently. "I should have realized some of this much sooner. What you're saying, what you're experiencing, is not at all unusual. And I agree. You need a change of scenery. Maybe an entirely different direction in life."

"You're glad to get rid of me?"

Moving in front of him, she leaned back against the edge of the desk. "Not at all. We'll miss you like hell. Physics teachers are hard to come by. Male teachers who have your kind of appeal to the students and the ability to connect without abusing the privilege... Well, you're the only one I've ever known."

She shrugged. "We'll find someone, or a couple of someones if we need to. I'm glad you told me what you're thinking about, Mason. Don't feel guilty—maybe you'll discover that your best option remains here at Hawkridge."

"Maybe I will." He got to his feet. "Thanks for your tolerance."

"No problem. And I'll talk with Nola later today, and try to get this issue with Zara worked out."

"Great." Mason nodded and turned to leave, shutting the door at his back. Before the lock quite clicked, however, he heard something hard slam against the wall within.

And he distinctly heard Jayne Thomas say, "Damn. Damn, damn, damn!"

He couldn't help grinning. It was nice to be wanted.

Chapter Eight

Friday afternoon, Nola stayed in her classroom grading papers long after the final bell had rung. She didn't want to take the work home with her—she wanted to spend the weekend sightseeing in the mountains and writing tests for each class to take at the end of the following week.

She jumped when someone knocked crisply on the frosted glass of her closed door. "Yes?" She'd been expecting Mason at any moment, after Wednesday's disaster with Zara.

But Jayne Thomas opened the door. "It's Friday afternoon, you know. You're supposed to be relaxing, recovering from the week."

Nola put down her red pen. "I'm almost to that point. I thought I'd get the grading done first, and then I could relax without any guilt."

"A good plan, in this administrator's view." Jayne sat on the student table nearest Nola's desk. "I spoke with Mason yesterday. He said Wednesday's session with Zara didn't go well but he wasn't sure why. I thought I'd see what you thought."

"I think that's a kind way of describing a total disaster."

"Could you fill me in on the details?"

"Zara acted badly. She was rude and completely uncooperative." Jayne started to say something, but Nola shook her head. "I wasn't rude, but I think uncooperative probably describes my behavior as well. Between the two of us, poor Mason didn't stand a chance."

"Is there a reason for this conflict? Something Mason doesn't know about?"

Nola explained about the session on Tuesday, about inviting Zara to stay for dinner. "I wanted a connection with her. And we were making progress, I think. But the conversation veered in an…uncomfortable…direction. I didn't know how to handle it, and I guess Zara felt rejected. The next day neither of us had recovered, and Mason got caught in the middle."

"Mason himself was the uncomfortable topic of conversation, I gather."

Nola felt a blush creep over her face. "I didn't want to talk about him like a teenager. If that's the kind of rapport that's called for…"

"No, it's not." Jayne sat for a moment in silence. "Zara is so starved for friendship, she probably crossed the student/teacher line without realizing it. You remembered, however, and that embarrassed her. I think you were more right than wrong in your handling of that situation." She looked up and caught Nola's gaze. "Wednesday, of course, you should have been the teacher again, oblivious to personal complications, focused solely on the task at hand."

She slid off the table. "But few of us are in such complete control of our feelings. And you and Zara are so much alike— cautious with your trust, self-reliant and yet lonely. I don't wonder you find yourselves in conflict."

Nola stirred in her chair. Jayne's assessment of her vulnerabilities hit hard. "I'm still not sure I can be an effective mentor for her. Maybe someone else could be more successful."

The headmistress shook her head. "No, we've embarked on this program and I think we'll persist. Keep trying—that's all we can do. You might explain to Mason that you and Zara had an argument." She saw Nola's horrified expression and smiled. "Without revealing the exact topic, of course. Make something up."

She went toward the door. "We'll see how Zara does on her first test in your class. If she's still utterly failing, then perhaps we'll reconsider. Now, finish your work and take off for the weekend." Before Nola could say goodbye, Jayne's footsteps receded down the hallway.

After finishing up the remaining few papers, Nola placed the textbooks she needed in her briefcase and left her classroom for the weekend. The sun had already dropped behind the treetops, leaving the campus in shadow, with a cool edge to the breeze. The sky was a clear, dusky blue and the weekend report promised good weather. She hoped to spend most of both days outdoors.

At the fork in the path that would take her directly to Pink's Cottage she hesitated, gazing toward the forest. To feel completely free of responsibility, she really should get things cleared up with Mason. Otherwise she'd be fretting about what she should say, what he would think, instead of simply enjoying her time off.

So rather than head straight for her cottage, she walked on toward the tree line and the hunting lodge beyond. Darkness fell like a curtain as soon as she stepped into the woods, but she could see the porch lights of Mason's house flickering between the trees up ahead, like a beacon drawing her home. She reached the stone wall surrounding the lodge grounds and pushed open the wooden gate.

At the creak of wood and the squeak of metal hinges, all hell broke loose.

Their sound reached her first—the cacophony of barking dogs, blended with yelps, howls and growls. Then the animals themselves arrived, all four of them racing toward her, mouths and eyes wide open. The first one landed with its paws on her stomach, knocking her back a step. The little one jumped at her, claws scraping down her slacks from knee to heel. A third body bowled into her from behind. The fourth slammed against the side of one knee and knocked her to the ground.

Arms crossed over her face, Nola felt all four of them pawing, sniffing, licking, scratching. They walked on her hair and across her chest and face. She tried to scream and got a mouthful of fur. Pushing them away appeared to be a game they enjoyed—each one simply returned for another shove. Finally she just lay still and played dead, hoping they'd give up and leave her alone.

Rescue came instead. "Angel! Gimp! Down, now!" That was Garrett's voice.

"Ruff, sit! Ready, sit! Stay!" Mason had arrived to witness the disaster. "Take them to the back, Garrett. Put them behind the fence and be sure the gate is locked."

Then his hands touched her face, her arm. "Nola? Nola, are you okay? Open your eyes. You're safe now."

Taking a small breath, she did as she was told. Mason leaned over her, his brows drawn together, his eyes dark with concern. He stroked her hair back from her forehead and ears with fingers that trembled.

"Say something," he pleaded. "Even if it's just to cuss me out for having such rotten dogs."

"You do have rotten dogs," she whispered.

"I know, I'm sorry." He slipped a hand under her shoulder. "Can you sit up? Are you hurt?" His gaze slid over her body. "I don't see any blood."

"I'm okay." Nola used her arms to push herself upright. "Just winded." She caught sight of the dirt on her clothes and skin. "And filthy."

"Damn, I am so sorry." He helped her to her feet. "Come inside and let's make sure you're okay, clean you up some."

For once, she didn't hesitate to lean on him. "I had a bag with me…"

He found the case right outside the gate. "I've got it. Now let me help you up the steps." His arm circled her waist and held her tight. A hand on her elbow kept her upright without any effort on her part. His body against hers was solid and warm and worth the price of being mauled by four stupid dogs.

Inside the house, Mason walked her to the kitchen and carefully placed her in a chair at the table. Moments later, a first-aid kit lay open on the counter and he was stroking her face with a soft, soapy washcloth.

"I think they recognized you as a friend." His fingers tilted her chin up, then he wiped her throat from jawline to collarbone. "And were glad to see you."

"So you don't need to worry about anyone breaking into your house," Nola commented. "The noise alone would scare off the most desperate burglar."

"That was the reasoning." He stepped behind her and removed her jacket. The next thing she knew, he was washing her hands and arms.

This had to stop. Her pulse had started to pound and she was having trouble catching her breath. If he noticed, if he knew...

She pulled back from his touch. "That's good, Mason. Thank you—I'm fine."

He sat in a chair in front of her, his knees almost touching hers. "Are you sure you're not scratched or cut somewhere? Did you check your ankles?" He glanced at her clothes. "I owe you a new shirt and slacks, that's for sure. And those shoes may never be the same."

Nola had already noticed the tooth marks on the toes of her Italian-leather loafers. "I'm okay. Really." Since he wasn't moving, she scooted her chair back and stood up. "If I could have a drink of water...?"

"Of course. I can offer something stronger, if you'd like. Beer? A glass of wine?"

The temptation to share a glass of wine with him almost conquered her. "Water will be fine. And I need to talk to you for a minute, if you're not busy."

He handed her a glass of ice water. "I'm at your service. Why don't we sit in the den, where we can be comfortable?"

"This won't take that long." Being comfortable with him was more than she could handle. "I just wanted to explain about Wednesday. With Zara. She and I had a—a disagreement Tuesday night. She left angry, I was mad at her and at myself for handling it badly, and we both brought that attitude with us to the session. I don't know about her, but I'll be more adult next time." She shrugged. "That's all I really wanted to say."

"You would think, after twelve years in a girls' school, not to mention earning a minor in child psychology, that I'd understand women." He shook his head. "But I'm not sure one hundred twenty years would be long enough."

Nola set the glass by the sink, noticing the homey feel of the kitchen, with its butcher-block counters and glass-fronted cabinets, the framed needlework hanging on the walls and the cheerful apple-print curtains at the windows. From the feminine feel, she felt certain Gail had been the cook and decorator in the house.

"I apologize for letting emotions get in the way of work," Nola said, turning to look at Mason. "I don't, usually."

He stood with his hands in his back pockets, his feet set apart and his legs braced. "I'm sure you don't."

She blinked in surprise. "I beg your pardon?"

"You seem to work hard at keeping your emotions as deeply buried as possible."

For a second she could only stare at him, until her brain caught up with the change of direction. "I don't want to have this conversation."

"Because you don't want to discuss emotions?"

Her internal alarm bells were going off, personal sirens blaring. "Because it's really none of your business."

"As I think you just pointed out, your emotions affect your work. That makes what you're feeling my business."

"I also said I won't let it happen again." She walked past him, toward the front of the house.

Tried to, anyway. As she passed, he caught her upper arm in a strong grip. Now they stood shoulder against shoulder, their faces, as they glared at each other, only inches apart.

"Emotions are necessary," Mason said in a low voice. "Especially for a teacher. If you don't allow yourself emotions, you can't empathize with the students. Effective teaching requires empathy. Especially at Hawkridge."

Nola set her teeth. "Then it's a good thing I'm only a substitute, isn't it?"

"It's a good thing there really is a heart beating behind that wall you've built around yourself."

She couldn't object, couldn't deny his analysis. "Mason, please…"

His dark brown eyes stared into hers a moment longer. Then his hand loosened, but only so that he could close his arms around her. And his lips covered hers.

She'd been kissed before, but never with anger, like this. Or desperation, or aching hunger. Mason's mouth was hot, and hard, tasting like nothing she'd ever known but had always craved. His hands held her tight, at waist and shoulder, molding her against the muscles of his chest, the bones of his thighs. She couldn't breathe.

But she could feel. Desire arced through her, streams of sparks racing across her skin, streaking through muscle and bone to swirl in her head and her breasts and her belly. She felt fear, because there was no control, nothing she could do to stop him…or herself, as response ignited and she began to kiss him back. Joy seeped out as tears from under her lowered lashes, because this was Mason, whom she had always loved, and she was finally, *finally* in his arms where she had always needed to be.

A door slammed somewhere in the house. Paws pounded across wooden floors. Garrett called, "Dad? Dad, where are you?"

Mason turned toward the back door leading to the sunroom, putting Nola behind him. "In the—" He cleared his throat, wiped a hand across his face. "In the den, son. Put the dogs up before you come in." That would give them a couple of minutes.

Turning, he found Nola wiping trembling fingers across her cheeks, combing them through her hair. She took a deep, shaky breath. Mason lifted a hand, and she flinched.

"Don't," was all she said. It was more than enough.

"Did Ms. Shannon leave?" Garrett stood in the doorway. "I wanted… There you are." He came into the room, looking up at Nola with a pleading face. "Did Dad ask you to dinner? He promised if I went to the doctor, took my medicine and stayed in bed that he would ask if you'd stay. Did he? Did you say yes?"

"Garrett—" Mason put a hand on his son's shoulder. "Tonight's not a good time."

Nola took another deep breath. "Sure, Garrett," she said, her voice sounding almost normal. "I'll be glad to stay." The glance she threw at Mason both defied and challenged him. "What are we having to eat?"

FORTUNATELY, there was a big steak in the refrigerator, potatoes in the cupboard and a bag of broccoli in the freezer. While Garrett showed Nola the menagerie, Mason pulled dinner together and set the table. He even opened a bottle of cabernet and poured a glass for the adults. Nola might not need it, but he certainly did.

When he went to the sunroom to fetch them, he found

Nola standing in front of Rattles's cage while Garrett explained the fine points of raccoon care.

"He has to get worm medicine and shots, just like dogs and cats. 'Course, he doesn't get out in the wild anymore, so he wouldn't pick up diseases from other raccoons. But we keep him vaccinated, just in case."

Nola's expression showed her interest, but Mason noted that she stood with her arms folded around her waist, restraining any urge she might have felt to reach out and touch. Or be touched.

"Does Rattles stay in this room all the time?" She glanced over her shoulder at Mason without actually acknowledging his presence.

"Dad built him a big outdoor cage for the summertime. We'll put him out pretty soon, I guess. He can't move around as much to stay warm, so we don't leave him outside all winter."

"But he'll never be able to go free?"

Garrett shook his head. "With only three legs, he'd be easy prey."

"How long do raccoons live?"

"Maybe seven or ten years, in the wild. Like this, he could live to be fifteen or even older." He dropped a carrot into the cage and they watched Rattles scurry to pick it up with his front paws. "But he's not a pet the way the dogs are. I don't play with him. The law says you can't keep wild animals like Rattles as pets."

"There are laws about that?"

"We had to get a license to have him at all. If you find a wild animal, like a raccoon or a skunk, a fox or a bear, you're supposed to turn them over to a person with a license right away. Dr. Milburn, the veterinarian, has a license."

"That's good to know if you live in the forest like this." She studied the habitats Garrett and Gail had created—the three turtle tanks, the gerbil community with its exercise wheel and tower maze, the snake boxes and mouse cages, Rattles's five-foot-square winter crate and the three-story rabbit hutch. "You have an amazing collection, Garrett. Thanks for sharing it with me. Have you read all of those?" She nodded at the floor-to-ceiling shelves of animal books.

"Most of 'em."

"Gail started reading him animal books when he was a baby," Mason said. "He was collecting bugs while he was still crawling, I think." He grinned over at Garrett. "Although I do believe he ate some of them."

"Gross," Garrett said.

Nola laughed. "I agree." Her arms relaxed, and her hands fell to her sides.

Mason congratulated himself on the small victory. "Luckily we don't have to eat insects for dinner, which is ready. You two wash your hands and come sit down."

Dinner passed with less tension than Mason had expected, maybe because of the wine, maybe because Garrett could talk nonstop for hours about his animals and all Nola and Mason had to do was listen. Nola allowed Mason to refill her wineglass once, and the three of them lingered at the table even after they'd finished the remainder of a package of chocolate-chip cookies.

By the time Mason turned on the dishwasher and wiped down the kitchen counter, nine o'clock had come and gone. "I should go," Nola said, sounding both regretful and horrified. "I never meant to stay so late."

Garrett yawned. "We usually watch a movie on Friday nights. You could stay and watch it with us, couldn't she, Dad? I was thinking about the first pirate movie. Have you seen it?"

Mason knew he didn't have to intervene.

Nola smiled and shook her head. "Thank you for the invitation, but I think I'd better go back to the cottage."

"Go put the movie in," Mason told his son. "I'm going to walk Ms. Shannon to her cottage."

"I'll wait for you," Garrett said.

"You don't have to do that," Nola protested at the same time.

Putting a hand on Nola's shoulder to direct her toward the front door, Mason looked at Garrett. "When we're out of the house, you can let the dogs out of their crates. And you should start the movie, because you'll probably be asleep before I get back."

For once, he got no argument. "Okay. 'Night, Ms. Shannon."

"Good night, Garrett. Thanks for showing me your zoo."

"Sure." He yawned again, and shuffled toward the dog room. "I'm ready, Dad," he called.

Mason was ushering Nola onto the front porch. "Go ahead," he called back and shut the front door.

When he turned around, Nola already stood at the bottom of the steps. "I can get home by myself," she insisted. "I don't think you should leave Garrett alone."

Mason joined her on the walk. "In less than ten minutes, Garrett and all the dogs will be piled together on the sofa, asleep. You've seen what happens when anyone comes near the house—intruders are not a problem. And it's a dark walk back to Pink's Cottage." He slipped his hand around her elbow and turned her toward the trees. "So don't try to change my mind."

To his surprise, she did as he suggested and walked through the woods beside him in silence. Once they moved away from the blink of the lodge lights, the night closed in around them.

"I can't see a thing," Nola's voice shook and her body echoed the tremor. "You could lead me off a cliff and I wouldn't know until it was too late."

"I won't do any such thing." Mason let go of her elbow to put his arm securely around her waist. "I know this path with my eyes closed, quite literally. And I have great night vision. I'll keep you safe."

"Promises, promises," she muttered.

But he could, in fact, see fairly well in the darkness, and his feet met all the expected slopes and turns in the path. He walked at an easy pace, and after a few minutes Nola relaxed enough to make the experience a stroll rather than a forced march.

"I would have expected crickets," she said. "And night birds."

"This is still early in the season. Later, in summer, it's almost too noisy some nights."

"I guess that's right. I don't remember as well as I thought I did."

Ahead of them, tree trunks were becoming visible against the sky. The landscaped lawns of the Manor weren't far away, but Mason chose not to mention the fact. "You really liked your time here, didn't you?"

He felt Nola nod. "This is a safe place. The girls may not realize it while they're students, but looking back, you're grateful for the chance to…to breathe. Figure out what you want, who you are."

"That's what we try to do."

"I'm not sure Zara—oh!" Nola lifted her head. "Am I imagining that light up ahead?"

The first of the lamps that lit the campus had come into view. "No, you aren't. We're back to civilization." Still, Mason didn't move his arm, didn't loosen his hold on her.

As they emerged from the trees, however, Nola took several side steps, putting a good portion of air between them. Then she stopped altogether.

"I appreciate your escort through the woods," she told him, without actually facing him. "I really can manage the rest of the walk on my own. You should go back to Garrett." Finally, she met his gaze. "Thanks for dinner, and everything."

She extended a hand—for him to shake, he presumed.

"Everything?" Mason took her hand in his. Then he took

a step, bending his elbow so that their bodies came together with their clasped hands in between. "Including the kisses?"

Nola looked down, and tugged halfheartedly at the hand he held.

"I'm not going to apologize this time," he told her. "In fact, I'm going to do something even worse." With his free hand, he cupped her chin. "I'm going to kiss you again."

She gasped, so her lips were parted when he put his mouth against them. Mason took full advantage of the opportunity, until his heart pounded and his body throbbed and he knew he'd lose control if he didn't stop. *Now.*

He stepped back abruptly, but managed to be gentle as he released Nola's hand. "Not going to apologize for that, either." He sounded as if he'd run the entire way from the cottage. Twice.

"Start walking," he told her. "I'll watch you until you're out of sight."

She gave a small laugh. "That will make me very self-conscious."

He shrugged. "Or I can walk with you and kiss you again at your front gate. And on your doorstep."

For a second, he thought—hoped—she'd accept.

"Good night, Mason," she said firmly, then did an about-face and walked away from him with long, purposeful strides.

He did as he'd promised, and watched until she disappeared behind a stand of fir trees. Finally, hands in his pockets, he wandered back down the path to the lodge. For the first time in years, he found himself whistling. The tune came to him automatically, some Broadway song Gail had enjoyed. Mason could remember her singing the words, "Almost like being in love…"

As predicted, Garrett and the dogs were piled together on the sofa, all of them snoring while the movie played. Stretched out in the recliner, Mason fell asleep to the sound of clashing swords. For the first time in years he slept the night through, and didn't stir until dawn, when Angel scratched at the door to go outside.

Chapter Nine

Having survived two strenuous tension-filled weeks of school, Nola decided she deserved a holiday. So on Saturday morning she borrowed one of the school cars and took herself sightseeing. After coffee and a luscious cinnamon roll at the bakery in Ridgeville, the small village near Hawkridge, she drove the winding, scary road to Boone and from there to Blowing Rock, where she spent the night at a quaint bed-and-breakfast inn with a glorious view of the mountains right outside her window.

Trouble was, while browsing small shops, looking at pottery or paintings or jewelry, she would find herself remembering the feel of Mason's arms around her, hard, strong, intrinsically trustworthy. Standing on the precipice of the Blowing Rock, where legend said an Indian princess had died for love, Nola thought about the nip of Mason's teeth on her lower lip, the taste of him on her tongue...

She'd been working on a mathematical proof Mason had assigned several weeks earlier, but still hadn't come up with the answer.

She stomped into his classroom and tossed her notebook in front of him on the desk, pretending to be mad. "You changed something, didn't you? Made it impossible to solve?

Just so you could get back at me for finishing the Gerard proof before you did."

He gave her that wide-eyed innocent look of his. *"Would I do something like that?"*

"Yes, you would." As he opened the notebook to thumb through the pages, she came around to stand beside him. *"So what am I doing wrong?"*

The gorgeous spring afternoon passed unnoticed as they reviewed her work, evaluating each step of the complicated analysis. Nola pulled over a chair and they sat side by side, thighs touching. Sunlight streamed in through the west-facing windows and then receded, leaving the room in shadow. Mason turned on the desk lamp without interrupting the flow of ideas.

Two-thirds of the way through her notebook, he said, *"Here you go. This is the problem."* He stood and turned to the blackboard, grabbing a piece a chalk from the tray. *"You've proved this."* From memory, he copied her equation on the board. *"But then you changed the value you were solving for—you skipped to this…"* he pointed to the line in her book *"…instead of going here."*

Frowning, Nola got to her feet and watched him write out the correct formula. *"You're right. Of course, that's it."* She grabbed his upper arm and shook it. *"Damn you, Mason. You're the one who's supposed to be wrong, not me!"*

Laughing, he punched her shoulder lightly with his fist. *"Should I apologize for being perfect?"*

At the instant of his touch, her mood changed. *"No."* Nola gazed into his face, the desire to tease yielding to a more urgent need. *"Don't apologize. Just…"* She took the step that brought her mouth within inches of his. *"Just kiss me."*

She kept her eyes open, saw passion flare in his dark brown gaze. He opened his mouth slightly, drew in a breath that sounded shaky. But he didn't move.

So she did. Easing up on her toes, using her grip on his arm for balance, Nola pressed her lips to his.

Mason shuddered. His mouth clung to hers, his fingers relaxed against her shoulder.

In the next instant, though, he took a stride back. "No," he said, his voice thick and harsh. "This is not going to happen."

"Are you all right?" A hand grabbed Nola's wrist. "You'd better step back."

Nola blinked, then looked at the white-haired older woman who still held on to her. "I'm sorry?"

"You were swaying, as if you might fall. Back up," the woman ordered, and actually pulled her away from the barrier. "You'll give me a heart attack if you do that again."

Face burning, Nola promised she would be fine and left quickly. She didn't know whether to laugh at the idea of herself swooning over Mason or simply run as far and as fast as possible.

Sunday morning, she lay in bed in the early light listening to church bells in the rain. She and Mason seemed to be repeating their history, but as equals this time. Even so, their relationship was no more reliable now than twelve years ago. Then, he'd brushed her off without a second thought, gone on to marry and start a family. She'd never, despite her adolescent fantasies, been part of his plans.

Now, she'd made her own plans—her life, her future, lay in Boston with Ted. Mason was lonely and, Nola was certain, starved for a woman's touch—a terrible foundation for any kind of dependable relationship. And Nola would settle for nothing less.

She arrived back at Hawkridge in the middle of Sunday afternoon, determined to reestablish her personal distance from Mason Reed. The morning's rain had refreshed the garden, where the pinks and pansies all lifted their bright, clean faces to the sun breaking through the clouds. After an hour's nap on the Victorian fainting couch in the parlor, Nola spread her textbooks and lesson plans on the dining table and got busy, outlining the work for the rest of the year and specifically detailing each day of the next two weeks for all her classes.

When the phone rang at seven, she was ready for a break.

"Your last excuse is gone," Ruth Ann Blakely said after a brief greeting. "We'll be expecting you for volleyball tomorrow afternoon."

Nola ran her hand through her hair. "What are you talking about?"

"Zara's come down with the flu—the same kind Garrett had. You won't be doing any tutoring this week, so there's no reason you can't play ball."

"Is she very sick?"

"I just took her to the infirmary. Her temperature is a hundred and two and she feels pretty miserable, but a dose of pain reliever and some TLC from Mrs. Ryan worked wonders. I left Zara asleep, curled on her side with her cheek pillowed on her hands like a cherub."

"Now, that's an interesting contrast."

"Isn't it? Anyway, we'll see you tomorrow at three-thirty. Call Mason and tell him he's expected, too." The line went dead without warning.

Call Mason?

Nola stomped around her cottage for an hour, muttering, swearing, wishing she had a punching bag. Or a plane ticket back to Boston. She did not want to play sports with the faculty, did not want the inevitable camaraderie, only to leave. She especially did not want to play with—or even worse, against—Mason.

In the end, though, she couldn't see any way to avoid it. And so she phoned him. "I have bad news."

"What's wrong?"

"Nothing serious. But Ruth Ann has summoned me to volleyball tomorrow. She's ordered you to be there, too."

"We can't. Zara—"

"Is in the infirmary with the flu."

After a pause, he muttered, "Damn."

"Exactly."

"Well, how bad can it be? We'll just fumble through and call it a day. It's only a game."

"Right."

"Zara will be better next week, and we'll go back to the regular schedule."

"I hope so."

"Two days out of our lives won't hurt."

"Yes, except…"

"Except what?"

She'd meant to tell him Friday night, until he'd distracted her. "Ruth Ann has also made both of us faculty advisers for the spring dance."

"No."

"You are the adviser on the decoration committee."

"No! That was Gail's department—I don't know the first thing about decorations."

"Me, neither. I'm working with the music committee."

Mason was silent for a moment. Then he issued an indictment of Ruth Ann, the school, the students and the dance that was both profane and hysterically funny.

"Exactly," Nola said, laughing until tears ran down her cheeks. "See you tomorrow at volleyball."

MONDAY AFTERNOON, Mason joined the other teachers in front of the net, those who weren't excused on account of age or advanced pregnancy, which was almost everybody.

Alice Tolbert slapped him on the back. "Good to see you out here, finally. Wish you were on my team, though. We need a power server. Not to mention someone who can actually return your serves."

Mason managed a grin. "It's been so long since I played, I doubt that'll be a problem."

"Son, all you need is the testosterone you got circulating in your body, and most of us females are defeated before we even get started." She winked at him. "On and off the volley-ball court."

He rolled his eyes. "Give me a break." But this time, the grin was easier.

Ruth Ann stood on the other side of the net. "Come on, Mason, get on the right team. We're setting up our battle plan."

"Yes, ma'am." Standing next to Kathy Burns, the art teacher, he concentrated on Ruth Ann's explanation of their rotation order, court positions and game strategy. Ruth Ann took her "just for fun" faculty sports very seriously.

When they broke to start the game, Mason took his position by the net and waved to Garrett sitting right behind the headmistress, then faced forward to look straight into Nola's blue eyes.

For the first time all day, he actually felt like smiling. "Well, hello. You're the best thing that's happened to me since breakfast."

"Not for long," she said, looking past him at Ruth Ann in the server's position. Mason heard the pop of the ball being put in play, caught a glimpse as it sailed over his head. On the other side of the net, Alice linked her hands in front of her and bumped the ball into the air. Gin Fisher, the biology teacher, sent it up again. And then Nola coiled, extended, reached...

And slammed the volleyball down on the ground beside him.

He swallowed the first word that came to mind. When her team had finished celebrating, he looked at Nola. "What was that?"

"A spike." She smiled at him. "I guess you don't forget some things."

"I guess not." He glanced at her dark red sweatpants, which had Harvard printed along the side seam. "You played in college?"

"Just a few months."

"Thank God," Mason said fervently. "If you'd played all four years, we'd never survive."

As it was, the battle was fierce. Between them, Mason and Ruth Ann could field just about anything that came over the net, even Nola's serves. But their teammates, some of the less athletic faculty members, weren't up to the challenge. Early in the game, Mason noticed Nola reducing the power of her hits, except when she aimed in his direction. The ball came at him full force, time and time again.

And that was all right, because he sent it back to her the same way. He'd learned to pull his punches, so to speak, in faculty volleyball games, because the players were teachers who just wanted a good time, not a team of well-conditioned men determined to win. With Nola across the net, however, he hit as hard as he could, knowing he'd get the ball back with equal energy. Man, it felt good.

At the end of the fourth game the score was tied, two-two, and they decided to play a tiebreaker. Unlike the regular games, where only the team serving could score, in this match every grounded ball earned a point. Even the tiebreaker ended up even, so the match came down to the last volley. Nola stood with the ball, ready to serve. Mason crouched in the center of the court, able to move up to the net, with Ruth Ann at his back.

Nola tossed the ball high and drew her arm back. Even before the hit, Mason knew it would come to him. He locked his hands, and bumped the ball, taking most of the force into his own body. "Linda," he yelled. "Set it up!"

Linda Butler, the French teacher, scurried into position. "Got it!"

Mason could have pushed in for the final hit. They would

win, because he'd place it as far from Nola as possible, at the weakest point on their team.

Instead, he stood back while Mary Franklin made the hit. She got the ball over the net—a miracle in itself—but without the power needed to reach Nola on the back row. Alice Tolbert bumped the ball, Gin set it up and Dee Hendricks knocked it back over.

Well, almost, anyway. The ball teetered on the canvas edge of the net and then dropped at Dee's feet.

"All right!" Ruth Ann came running from the back row, slapping hands and backs and butts. "Way to go, guys. Great win."

From Nola's side of the court came a chorus of commiseration.

"That's okay."

"Don't worry about it."

"We played a good, hard game."

Amidst the comforting hugs, Mason noticed one person conspicuously absent. He glanced around and saw Nola at the bleachers, rummaging through a sports bag.

As he approached, she pulled out a towel and buried her face in clean white terry.

He propped a foot on the bench to stretch his hamstrings. "Good game."

Her head came up out of the towel. "You, too." She blotted her neck and arms. "Excellent choice you made, there at the end. I wasn't sure how to play it."

He shrugged and switched to stretching the other leg. "Maybe I just shirked the responsibility for winning or losing."

"At least this way no one resents you." She stuffed the towel back in her bag, pulled the strap over her shoulder and picked up her briefcase with the other hand. "See you later."

"Wait. I'm headed that way." He wasn't about to let her walk off alone.

By means of careful steering, he eased Nola back into the group of teachers still lingering on the court to review the moves of the game. Somebody had brought a cooler filled with ice and soft drinks, and Mason made sure Nola ended up with one in her hand. He couldn't force her to talk, of course, but she was polite enough to listen and to respond if addressed.

When the crowd finally began to disperse, he allowed her to drift toward Pink's Cottage. As Garrett raced ahead of them toward the tree line, Mason glanced at Nola, walking beside him. "That wasn't so bad, was it?"

She stared straight ahead. "I don't mind talking to people."

"If you can't avoid it."

"I'm quiet."

"You're reclusive."

"Says the person who had to be threatened into playing today."

"Did you get hassled by the team at Harvard when you played?"

Nola blew out an irritated breath. "Something else I don't want to talk about."

"Is that why you didn't want to play?"

They'd almost reached the cottage gate. "It wasn't a big deal." She gave a careless shrug. "I find people distracting, anyway. I need privacy to focus on my work, and I work long hours, which doesn't allow much time for socializing."

"You're very good at rationalizing."

"You're very good at interfering." She went into the garden and slammed the gate between them. She spun around to face him. "Why won't you leave me alone?"

"Hell if I know." Mason didn't look around to see if anyone was watching. He just put a hand at the back of her head, pulling her close enough to give her a kiss. A kiss that started out casual, even sarcastic, but quickly surged out of his control.

He stepped back as Nola broke away. Both of them were breathing heavily.

"Maybe that's why," he said.

"A physical…reaction…is no reason to disrupt my life."

Mason barked a laugh. "I wish that's all this was." Then he turned and ran, as if his life depended on it.

THE FIRST MEETING for spring dance volunteers took place in the library on Tuesday afternoon. Each committee was assigned its own table—music and decorations were, Nola was grateful to see, at opposite ends of the room.

Hawkridge tradition held that the theme of the dance was always chosen by the previous year's organizers, and then kept a secret until the faculty sponsor opened the envelope containing the theme at the first volunteer meeting.

"I hope it's something about magic," a student at Nola's table said. "We could do fairies and wizards and—"

"That's dumb." The girl beside her wore her hair in dreadlocks and bore scars on her face and ears—and who knew where else—from numerous piercings. "We should do a Caribbean theme, have reggae music and fried conch to eat. Not to mention rum punch." She glanced at Nola, who gave her a smile instead of the shocked reaction she'd expected.

"Here we go." Standing at the front of the room, Ruth Ann held up a plain business envelope. "And this year's spring dance theme is…" She drew out a slip of paper and winced. "Country Daze?"

Absolute silence greeted her words, followed a moment later by an explosion of protests.

"That's mean!"

"Like in country music? Gross!"

"Can we choose our own theme?"

"I won't listen to country music. That's all there is to it."

Ruth Ann raised a hand, and the girls quieted somewhat.

"If we absolutely can't come up with any ideas to make Country Daze work, I guess I can tell Ms. Thomas we have to change tradition and come up with something different." She blew out a deep breath. "I hate to admit we don't have enough imagination, but maybe that's the way to go."

Nola looked at the other teachers seated with their committees. They all appeared to have taken a hands-off approach to this crisis—even Mason sat silent, arms folded, watching the disaster without contributing.

Didn't they understand how important this dance was to the girls? After a year of studying, of seeing the same people every day, every night and all weekend, the spring dance was a moment of magic, a chance for each of them to shine. For one evening, they weren't just a bunch of girls shipped off to the mountains because no one could handle them elsewhere. For a few hours, they could be stars.

She stood up. The room quieted, and everyone looked at her in surprise. "The Country Daze theme is a challenge," Nola said, "but couldn't we work with it? There are some good things about being out in the country—"

"Yeah, right." A girl at Mason's table rolled her eyes. "Eating watermelon and spitting out the seeds."

After the laughter had died down, Nola said, "That's probably not something we want to encourage for the spring dance. But what about the bright stars you can see out in the country at night? Stack bales of straw around the dance floor, but drape them with pretty fabric to make places to sit. As for the music—" she turned to look at her own committee "—we don't have to play strictly country music. We can ask the deejay to mix the songs you choose with some popular country hits. There are crossover artists, you know." She named a couple of singers and got a few sighs and swoons in response. "You see, some of the music you enjoy just might fit the theme."

"In other words, make the country theme special. Romantic." Ruth Ann nodded. "I'm seeing possibilities here."

A girl on the refreshments committee raised her hand. "What about food? Corn on the cob and fatback?"

"How about chocolates shaped like animals?" someone at her table said. "Cows, horses, chickens, and stuff like that?"

"You could get those potato sticks instead of chips," someone called across the room. "That would look like straw."

"And punch that looks like cider."

"Animal crackers?"

"Vegetables and dip."

"Crackers shaped like goldfish?"

Nola sat down again. Conversations were starting up around each table, plans being written down. The girls beside her were comparing notes on their favorite singers, checking the Internet for those who showed up on both rock and country radio stations, making a list of the music they would want to hear.

Someone took hold of Nola's shoulders from behind. "You're the woman who saved the spring dance," Ruth Ann said softly in her ear. "Good job."

"No problem." Smiling, Nola watched Ruth Ann visit each of the committees in turn. Then suddenly, without intending to, she met Mason's intent gaze. Across the length of the room and all the heads between them, he sent her a look that heated her cheeks and hurried her heartbeat. He might as well have kissed her in public.

And she was terrified to find herself wishing he would.

NOLA VISITED the infirmary after Wednesday's volleyball game. She found Zara dressed and sitting on the edge of her unmade bed.

"You must be feeling better."

"Yeah, I go back to my room in a few minutes." She punched the pillow beside her. "I can't wait to be with my own stuff."

"I can imagine." A glance outside showed her a bird's-eye view of the volleyball court. "You could have watched the faculty game from here."

"I did." Zara waved a hand at her sweatpants and sneakers. "You're pretty good. So's Mason."

"That would be Mr. Reed, right?"

Zara shrugged. "Whatever. Your team beat his today."

"So we're even. They won on Monday."

"Guess we'll have to back off on the tutoring so you can keep playing."

"Not so fast." Nola shook her head. "I think we can manage to do both. You'll come watch the games, then we'll go to the lodge for tutoring."

"I don't need to watch the games."

"No, you don't. But you might have fun if you do."

Zara shrugged a shoulder.

"You might get a chance to talk with other girls."

"What difference does that make? I'll never see them again after graduation."

Nola couldn't argue. "Well, it gives you an excuse to get outside, anyway."

"Don't need one."

"You could keep Garrett company."

After a moment, she said grudgingly, "I guess so."

Feeling wearier than usual, Nola gave up on her attempt at bringing good cheer. "Anyway, I'm glad you're recovering. We'll start back with the tutoring on Monday afternoon, okay?" She turned toward the door.

"If I have to."

Her whiny tone, on top of the barrage of negative reactions, finally broke Nola's control. She spun back to look at Zara. "What does it take to get through to you?"

The girl stared at her with a blank expression. "Huh?"

"You've got people here turning themselves inside out to

improve your situation. The headmistress, Mason Reed, Mrs. Ryan, me…"

Zara rolled her eyes. "Give me a break. You all just want me to go away."

"We want to give you the tools to make a decent life for yourself."

One hand waved the idea away. "I'm fine."

"How can you be fine? You stand in danger of leaving Hawkridge without a diploma. You can't get into college and your job options are limited. On top of which, your resentful, sarcastic attitude pushes away anyone who might try to do you a favor or—God forbid—make friends."

"Oh, and you're Ms. Personality?" Zara stood up, her hands propped on her hips. "Do you know what it's like to sit in class for forty minutes every day with a teacher who never smiles? No jokes, no personal info—just straight math until you think you could scream with boredom."

Nola stood speechless for a moment, choking on a combination of anger and embarrassment. "I have a job to do."

"You're a *person* with a job to do," Zara countered. "That means occasionally acting like you're human."

"I didn't hear an alarm," Mason said from the doorway. "But somebody in here is definitely all fired up. What's going on?"

Chapter Ten

Garrett peered around Mason from behind, then popped into the room before his father could grab him. "Hi, Zara. Dad said I gave you the flu. I'm sorry."

Zara shifted her gaze from Nola's face and gave Garrett a smile. "It's okay. I got to miss three days of school."

"Yeah, that's the good part." Garrett sat on the end of the bed. "I didn't like feeling tired all the time and achy, though."

"Nope, that sucks." Zara got to her feet. "This is a nice party and all, but I think I'll head back to the dorm." She made a brave show of walking out, but her steps wavered as she reached Mason. He caught her arm with one hand and felt her weight sag.

"Maybe you should stay here," he said with a glance at Nola. "Another night in the infirmary won't hurt."

A brisk step sounded at his back. Mrs. Ryan cleared her throat. "Unfortunately, I've got two more girls who are sick and I need this bed. Zara's been fever-free for twenty-four hours. I've given her instructions and told the resident on her hall what to do." She glanced over her shoulder at another student coming through the infirmary door—white-faced, heavy-eyed and hunched over.

"Make that three girls who are sick. Mr. Reed, could you

and Ms. Shannon walk Zara to her room? Garrett can stay here with me until you get her settled."

Mason had never, in twelve years, entered the dormitories, and he didn't want to do so now. Nola was looking at Zara with all the horror she felt showing in her face—clearly, she preferred to keep her distance, as well, though for different reasons.

And Zara was looking from Nola's face to Mason's and back again, as if they both carried the bubonic plague.

"We'll do that," Mason said. "Hang out here for a few minutes, Garrett. I'll be right back." Keeping one hand around Zara's upper arm, he waved Nola to the girl's other side. "She might need both of us."

Lips pressed together, Nola did as he asked. Without a word, they escorted Zara out of the infirmary and through the glass-walled walkway connecting the Manor to the dormitory building. No one spoke as they rode the elevator up. In the third-floor hallway, Zara nodded to the left.

"I'm this way."

"Man on the hall!" someone yelled. Doors slammed in response, but there were still a number of open rooms along the way. Curious stares followed them down to the last room on the right, where a construction-paper sign said simply, Z. Kauffman.

Zara reached for the handle and pushed the door open, then pulled her arm from Mason's grasp. "I'm here now. Thanks." Stepping inside, she flicked the overhead light on. Mason glimpsed a spartan space—bare walls, empty surfaces, a neatly made bed. Then Zara said, "Good night," and shut the door in his face.

"Well." Hands in his pockets, he took a couple of steps back. "I hope she'll be okay."

When he looked at Nola, he found her gazing along the now-empty hallway. "Believe it or not, I do, too."

He waited until they had the elevator to themselves before asking, "What happened before I arrived?"

"It's not important."

"To have upset you—and Zara—this much, I'd say it was damn important."

The elevator door slid open and Nola exited into the deserted walkway. "Don't worry about it, Mason. I'll—"

He took her arm and turned her around to face him. When he saw the distress and despair in her face, though, his irritation vanished.

"Oh, Nola." Loosening his grip, he let his hand slide down her arm to catch at her wrist. "Listen, why don't you come with me and Garrett into town for dinner? There's a half-decent pizza place we usually hit on Wednesdays. They have a salad bar, too," he said quickly as she opened her mouth, "in case you can't abide pizza."

That won him a near smile. "Maybe some other time," Nola said. "I'm really tired, and I've got tests to grade. Thanks for the invitation." She tugged gently at his hold, and he released her.

But as she walked away, Mason decided to push the issue. "Friday?" he called.

She stopped and looked back over her shoulder. "Friday what?"

"Dinner. On Friday."

She pursed her lips for a second, and he knew she was annoyed that he wouldn't let go.

"Mason—"

"You said another time. So…Friday?"

She blew out a frustrated breath. "Okay, Friday." The tone implied she'd agree to anything just to get rid of him.

"Great. Happy grading."

She waved without looking back as she went through the double doors to the main staircase. Mason would take the opposite direction to pick up Garrett at the infirmary. But for a minute he simply stood there, rocking back and forth from his heels to his toes, enjoying his achievement.

He'd just made a date with Nola Shannon. She didn't know it was a date, of course—she thought Garrett would be there, thought they'd end up at a pizza place suitable for ten-year-olds.

The café he had in mind catered to more sophisticated tastes. Though the atmosphere was casual, the wine list was not. For the first time in three years, Mason planned to enjoy terrific food and a decent bottle of wine with a woman he wanted to talk to about everything under the sun except work.

He thought Friday night might just be the first night of the rest of his life.

WALKING HOME after visiting Zara, Garrett realized his dad was in a really good mood. Maybe playing volleyball made him feel better. Or maybe Ms. Shannon did.

Garrett thought they liked each other. Not like old friends, though. Since the night she'd eaten dinner with them, his dad had been less grumpy. He'd been playing fetch with the dogs and working with Ruff and Ready on their manners. Maybe she'd be coming to dinner again soon.

That was okay with Garrett. Ms. Shannon seemed like the kind of lady who could be nice to kids. Everybody loved babies, but not everybody liked kids. Especially boys. His teacher this year, for one. School was kinda tough when your teacher only talked to the girls.

So of course that's what his dad wanted to talk about that night at dinner. He'd made spaghetti and meat sauce, Garrett's favorite, with garlic bread and a salad. "Your report card leaves a lot to be desired, you know. Four Cs, a D and an NS— not satisfactory—on conduct? What's going on, Garrett?"

"Nothing," Garrett said around a mouthful of noodles.

For that, he got a lifted eyebrow. "Don't talk with your mouth full." His dad twirled some spaghetti onto his fork, but he didn't put it into his mouth. "I know you're smarter than this report shows."

Yeah, but the teacher was dumb. "I try," he mumbled. "Sometimes, I just forget the answers."

Crumbling a piece of bread, his dad stared at him. "You don't like school, do you?"

This, he could tell the truth about. "Not much. I'd rather be outside."

"Or maybe you're just not getting the help you need there." His dad took a sip of wine. Garrett didn't know how he could stand the stuff. "Listen, I'm going to be taking some trips in the next few weeks."

"Can I go? Can I go?" Garrett loved traveling. He wanted to visit every zoo in the United States.

"I don't think that would help your grades much." His dad shook his head. "Granddad and Grandma Chance will be coming to stay with you."

"Oh, yeah?" That wasn't too bad—they always brought him presents. "Where are you going?"

"California, Arizona, Washington state."

"What for?"

This time his dad put the fork in his mouth and chewed. Slowly. Then he took another drink of wine.

"What for, Dad?"

His dad put the fork down and folded his arms on the table in front of his plate. "I'm looking for a new job, Garrett."

That took a minute to sink in. "You mean—you want to move? Leave here?"

"Maybe."

"Why?"

"I need a change. New place, new people. I think maybe you do, too."

Garrett pushed himself and his chair back from the table. "No, I don't. I like it here. School's okay, Dad. Honest."

His dad held up a hand. "Don't get upset, son. All I'm doing right now is going to visit a few other schools. No one's offered me a job, and I haven't made any decisions."

"But…" Garrett didn't know what to say. He'd asked his mom for help—was this part of her plan? Or was this the deadline he had to beat? "I don't want to move."

"We're not moving anytime soon. Not before summer, anyway." His dad got up, came over and pushed him back to the table. "Eat your supper and do your homework. It's a regular night, Garrett, like every other one. I just thought I'd let you know what was coming up in the next couple of weeks."

Garrett crossed his arms over his chest. "I'm not hungry. Can I go to my room?"

His dad blew out a big breath. "Sure. I'll save your plate, in case you're hungry later."

In his room, Garrett threw himself facedown on the bed. He wouldn't be hungry later. He might never be hungry again, if what he feared came true.

"Did you hear that, Mom? You gotta do something. Ms. Shannon would be a good wife—help him out with her. Quick. Or else…"

Garrett squeezed his eyes shut, and tried to shut his brain off, too. He didn't want to think about what came after "or else…"

BY THE TIME Nola reached Pink's Cottage, she'd recovered enough presence of mind to realize that Friday-night pizza with the Reeds, father and son, would be a mistake.

After dinner, she called Mason to tell him so. "I don't think it's a good idea."

"Why not?"

Why did he have to be so difficult? "Because I'd be seen leaving campus with you. The girls would misunderstand."

"You're not allowed a dinner in town now and then?"

"You know what I mean, Mason."

He was silent for a few seconds. "Well, then, take one of the school cars and drive yourself. We can meet in town, with nobody the wiser."

His simple solution left her almost no reason to refuse. She couldn't possibly tell him the truth—that she was afraid she'd enjoy an evening with Mason and his son far too much for her own peace of mind. Pretending they were a real family would be so easy.

"Nola? What do you think?"

Trapped. "That sounds like a reasonable compromise. Where is this pizza place?"

"The directions are a little complicated. Let's meet up at city hall about seven and go on from there."

"Okay. I'll see you then. Tell Garrett I'm looking forward to hearing more about his animals."

"Sure."

Then all she had to do was get through forty-eight hours without letting her mind wander to what she should wear, how long they might actually take to share a pizza, what she and Mason could talk about without ignoring Garrett too much, what she would say if someone mistook them for a couple with their son...

"Stop it!" she told herself sternly on Friday morning, clenching her fingers in her hair and pulling hard to make the point. Twelve hours to go, and she was daydreaming like a teenager instead of getting ready for her Friday classes. Her emotions were making a fool of her, just as she'd expected.

What she didn't expect was to see Zara in her second-period class. "It's good to have you here again," Nola said when the girl answered her name during roll call. "I hope you're feeling much better."

"I'm okay," Zara said—yet another surprise. Though she

avoided making eye contact, the simple response seemed to be progress. Only days ago, Nola felt sure a shrug would have been the girl's response.

"We've been working on word problems this week," she told Zara. "The paper I'm passing out has four problems for everyone to work on individually for the next thirty minutes. Then we'll go over them together so you can see how your solution compares to mine."

She moved around the room during that half hour, making herself available for questions. When she saw a girl looking frustrated, she went to offer help. After about twenty-five minutes, she glanced at the back of the room and saw Zara sitting with her head propped on one hand, while the other hand bounced a pencil against the desk.

Nola went to stand by Zara's desk. "How's it going?"

The girl shook her head. "I don't get this stuff."

"What have you done so far?" Nola slid the problem sheet away from the blank piece of notebook paper underneath. "Oh. Well, I'm not surprised, since you haven't been here all week. Maybe you'll pick up some tricks as we go through the problems in class." She looked at the rest of the girls. "Who would like to show us her solution for the first problem?"

Monday, she'd had no volunteers. But today, three girls raised their hands. "Great. Each of you can claim some space on the board and show us your work."

The bell ending class rang just as they finished the last problem. Nola assigned homework from the textbook and then said, "Have a good weekend." They all rushed out so fast, she doubted she'd been heard.

"Zara?" She reached the door just as the girl hurried after her peers. "Did you figure things out a bit?" Zara shook her head and tried to keep going.

But Nola reached out and cupped a hand around her upper arm, slowing her down. "Can you come back here after school this afternoon? I'll catch you up on the week and you'll be able to understand the weekend's homework."

Zara shrugged out of her hold. "I thought I didn't have to start tutoring again until Monday."

"You'll be that much further behind. I thought…"

"I gotta go. I'll be late for English." Before Nola could protest, she'd disappeared into the crowd.

So much for the personal touch, Nola decided, and returned to her room for third-period geometry. The classes and the minutes flew by, and then the final bell rang at three o'clock. In four hours, she would meet Mason and Garrett for dinner.

To calm her nerves she walked all the way to Hawk's Ridge, which was deserted on this warm April afternoon. The mountains vibrated with a thousand different spring greens, and the valley was carpeted with the same lush shades. She could see the white spire of a church in Ridgeville and a gray ribbon of road winding in that direction.

Three hours.

At five she stepped into the shower, created by an old-fashioned handheld nozzle attached to the claw-foot tub in the cottage bathroom. Her hair took almost no time to dry and almost as little to style. She'd decided on her clothes the day before—a pair of jeans, a white shirt and a sweater she couldn't resist because its color echoed the clear blue mountain sky. Dressing took only minutes, and makeup, a few more. She didn't need to look polished for Garrett. And Mason…well, he remembered her as a teenager with acne and stringy hair. Anything would be an improvement.

Two hours.

In desperation, she sat down with the research she'd avoided since arriving at Hawkridge. She needed a distraction—what could be better than the complex series of equations that comprised this new project? Pencil in hand, she began with her premise. "Let K be a finite field. Let I represent…"

When the phone rang, she gasped and jumped, dropping her pencil. Her heart pounded as she picked up the receiver. "Hello? Yes?"

"Nola?"

"Hi, Mason. Is something wrong? Garrett's not sick again, is he?"

"Uh, no. I was just wondering if you'd stood me up."

"But it's—" She looked at her watch. Seven-forty. "Oh, damn! I'm so sorry. I was working and completely lost track of the time. I'll leave right now. Unless…" She squeezed her eyes shut. "Would you rather just go on and eat? We could make it another time."

"Not on your life." She could hear laughter in his voice. "I'm waiting for you right here in the parking lot. Get in the car, Nola Shannon. Drive carefully, and I'll see you in about twenty minutes."

Nola HAD SEEN the Ridgeville City Hall on her explorations over the previous weekend—a brick rectangle surrounded by pine trees, rhododendrons and dogwoods. The parking lot sat to one side, and as she turned in she could see Mason leaning against the front bumper of the SUV.

"I am so sorry," she said as soon as she stood up out of the car. "I—"

He held up both hands. "Stop right there. No apology necessary. You were caught up in your work. Let's just get the evening started." Opening the door beside him, he ushered her in. "Have a seat."

A glance inside the car showed her an empty vehicle. "Where's Garrett?"

Mason took a deep breath. "I have to confess, I've been somewhat deceptive. Garrett won't be joining us."

She backed up a step. "Is he okay?"

"He's fine and, I imagine, enjoying his friend Jason's

birthday party. A sleepover," he added. "I'll pick him up tomorrow morning about ten."

Panic clawed at her chest. "Did you know about the party when you asked me to come out for pizza tonight?"

In the twilight, his gaze was hard to read. "Yes, I did. I knew you wouldn't come if I simply asked you for a date."

Nola clenched her fists. "You were right." Her brain ordered her to execute an immediate about-face, then stomp back to her car and drive away.

But her body, under some other control, refused to obey. She stared at Mason as brain warred with—okay, with heart. "I should leave," she said finally. "That wasn't fair."

"I know." He smiled at her. "But I'm hoping you won't. Since Wednesday, I've been looking forward to dinner with you."

And really what could she do, when the twinkle had come back to his eyes and the smile widened into his delicious grin?

"Just this once," she told him, taking her seat in the SUV.

"We'll see." He winked at her gasp of outrage. "You might discover that you like being with me too much to stop."

As he walked to the driver's side, Nola blew out a frustrated breath. Was the man blind? Liking his company was *not* part of the problem!

"That's the pizza parlor." Mason nodded to a brightly lit trading post–style building on the right side of the street. "Surprisingly good, especially if you like the deep-dish version."

"I prefer New York pizza—thin, crisp crust, not too much cheese."

"What do you put on it?"

"Vegetables, mostly. Sometimes sausage. Are you an all-the-meat-you-can-carry fan?"

"Garrett likes pepperoni, so I usually get pepperoni." He shrugged. "Gail liked mushroom-and-black-olive pizza."

Nola shifted in her seat so she could watch his profile. "But what's your choice? If you went out for pizza alone, how would you order?"

He laughed, and ran a hand over his face. "Does anybody go out for pizza alone?"

"I do."

"Okay. If I ordered my own pizza, I would ask for…" He tapped the wheel with his fingers, thinking. "Fresh tomatoes, fresh mozzarella cheese and Italian sausage. How's that?"

She nodded. "Sounds good to me. I might add some fresh basil."

"Yeah. And a bottle of Chianti. With Sinatra playing in the background."

"Do you know of a place like that in Ridgeville?"

"As a matter of fact, I do." He turned into another parking lot and stopped the car. "This place was a filling station back in the forties and fifties. I'm told you could pull up under the portico and get your car gassed, your windows washed and your oil checked, then drive off with an ice-cold cola in a small green bottle and a bag of roasted peanuts."

Nola squinted at the building as they walked toward it. "Hard to imagine. But then, I don't drive much." The portico had been closed in with windows and cushioned benches running along the walls to create a comfortable lobby.

"Why not?" Mason walked behind her as the hostess led them to a table. Nola was profoundly aware of the hand he placed lightly against the small of her back. "Don't you ever get the urge to go for a long drive in the country?"

"That might be one of the disadvantages of Hawkridge. You can't go anywhere, so you don't think about getting your driver's license when most teenagers do. I finally decided I should, in order to be self-sufficient. But I can walk from my apartment to my office, so I really don't need a car. These days I spend most of my time indoors or on the subway."

"You said you used to wander the woods when you were here."

"I got busy." She shrugged. "And I guess if I couldn't be in the mountains, I decided I'd just give up the outdoors more or less completely. Boston's not exactly a wilderness."

A glance at Mason showed him with his elbows braced on the table and his chin propped on his laced fingers, studying her. "What else did you give up when you left Hawkridge?" he asked gently.

You, was the answer that came immediately to mind, but she wouldn't voice the thought. "Mrs. Werner's rolls. I can already tell, from the fit of my jeans, that I've eaten too many of them since I came back."

He made a show of leaning to the side to check out her legs. "I just happened to notice the fit of your jeans, and I'm saying you have nothing to worry about."

The rough edge to his usually smooth voice gave her goose bumps.

She was grateful when their server chose that moment to arrive. Mason consulted her, then ordered a bottle of Chianti to accompany the small appetizer pizza they'd agreed to share.

"We forgot the Italian sausage," she reminded him.

"I'll have steak for dinner. Or lamb," he said, studying the menu. "Or pork. This all sounds good. I feel like I haven't eaten a decent meal in years." He looked up, his smile wry, his eyes sad. "Come to think of it, that's probably true. I'm not much of a cook."

Nola wanted to avoid talking about Gail. She would have preferred to deflect his reference with some light comment that sent them down a different path.

But she suspected this was one of the reasons he'd wanted to have dinner alone with her. They needed to talk about their lives.

The server filled their wineglasses, and Nola took a sip. "Very nice," she told Mason, and drank again. Then she sat back and looked at him across the table. "You've had a hard three years, being a single parent. Was Gail a good cook?"

"She was a traditional southern girl, raised to fry chicken and bake corn bread. She made a mean deviled egg and dynamite potato salad." Mason chuckled. "Before she got sick, I had put on a few pounds myself. Once she couldn't really cook anymore, the weight melted away."

"Do you have a picture of her?"

To Nola's surprise, he shook his head. "I've never been the picture-carrying kind. Gail kept scrapbooks, and most of our photographs went into those. Garrett's got a framed picture by his bed, and we have a family shot in the den." He picked up his glass and drank deep. "For a long time, I couldn't look at them."

"I remember she was pretty."

"Oh, yes. Even at the end, when she'd gotten so frail, she was still lovely. Reddish-brown hair and hazel eyes, creamy skin with freckles. She always complained about her figure, especially her hips, but I told her she was a cozy armful." He stared into his wine, which sloshed from side to side as he twisted the stem of the glass between his fingers.

"When she died, she only weighed about ninety pounds. A machine breathed for her, a machine fed her, kept her heart going. I knew she was tired but I kept talking, begging her to hold on. A transplant would be available any day. Any hour. She just had to wait long enough."

He shook his head. "But that night…I gave up for a minute. I stopped hoping. I put my head down on the bed and fell asleep."

Nola put her right hand over his left. "You can't blame yourself for being exhausted."

"I fell asleep," he said, "and she died. The alarm woke me up, the nurses coming in, the lights and noise and bustle. Of course they couldn't save her."

Mason sighed. "Three hours later, a transplant became available."

"I'm so sorry."

Without warning, he turned his palm up, so that his fingers, strong and warm, gripped hers.

"I'm the one who should apologize." He used his free hand to slap his own cheek. "I'm pretty sure the first rule in dating is, 'Don't talk about the last woman you dated.' Loved. Married. Whatever."

He released her hand in time for the server to set their appetizer on the table between them. For several minutes they ate silently, enjoying the flavor of their pizza and recovering their composure.

After his third slice of pizza and a second glass of wine, Mason sat back with folded arms. "Now it's your turn. How many broken hearts lie in your wake? Are you in the process of breaking one now?" He picked up his glass and made a silent toast in her direction.

"Besides mine, that is."

Chapter Eleven

Nola's smoky-blue eyes widened as his question registered. Her lips parted in surprise just as the server—damn him—stepped up to the table.

"Would you care to order your main courses now?"

Mason almost said, "I'd like your roasted head on a platter, surrounded by carrots, onions and potatoes." Instead, he bit his tongue and waited for his flustered date to gather her wits and ask for red snapper en papillote. After ordering lamb chops with garlic mashed potatoes, he looked at Nola again.

"Yet another unconscionable question on my part. Are you going to answer this one?"

Small salads arrived, delaying her response yet again. "I've had several relationships," Nola said finally. "Nothing very important or long-lasting."

Mason bit down on a crouton. "Then I would say those Ivy League guys aren't as smart as they think they are."

She stared at her plate. "No. They were interested in sex, or in my money, or in some kind of status they thought I could give them. But I don't like being used." One shoulder lifted in a shrug. "Ted is different."

"Ted?" He couldn't say another word—his mind had gone blank.

"Ted Winfield," Nola said, pushing lettuce leaves around with her fork. "We met in graduate school. He's tenure-track, Napoleonic history. We, um…"

With great care, Mason set his fork on the table. "You're engaged?"

She shook her head. "N-no."

"Dating seriously?"

"Not exactly."

"Sleeping together?"

Her gaze jerked up to his. "No! I mean, I wouldn't have…"

Mason found he could breathe again. "But he's interested, is that what you're saying?"

"I believe we could have a successful partnership."

"Ah." Relaxing, Mason eased back in his chair. This Winfield—not to mention the relationship Nola described between them—sounded pretty bloodless. If the guy wanted Nola, he should have staked a claim. As it was, Mason considered the field wide open. But not for long.

In the meantime, he moved the conversation into less personal territory. More food arrived. They traded lamb for snapper and agreed that they'd both chosen well. Nola decided on chocolate for dessert, while Mason ordered his favorite, gingerbread with lemon sauce and ice cream. Both servings were too big to finish and would go home in small foil boxes. But Mason wasn't ready for the evening to end. "Would you like some port? Cognac?"

Nola gazed at him in surprise. "How did you know?"

"Know what?"

She glanced around and then leaned forward, as if revealing a secret. "I'm an after-dinner-drinks fanatic."

He grinned. "That makes two of us. Come with me."

Once he'd pulled back her chair, he took her hand and led her to the lounge, where he'd originally planned to have drinks before they ate. Flames flickered in the fireplace, warming the cool spring night. Cozy sofas and deep chairs surrounded small tables where a few couples were gathered to listen to piano jazz from the baby grand in the corner.

Nola sipped her port slowly. Seated beside her on a small couch in the corner, Mason sloshed his scotch and took a swallow every now and then, extending the evening as long as possible. They relaxed into the soft cushions and somehow their knees came into contact, then their hips. He was quite aware of her warmth, the rise of her breasts with each indrawn breath, the graceful movement of her slender hands. When she'd finished her port he took her glass and set it on the table, then linked her fingers with his.

And all the time they talked, about math, about physics and airplanes and what had happened to the world in the last twelve years—computers and politics and medical advances, movies and music and the demotion of the planet Pluto.

They were still wrangling over the issue when the bartender approached. "I gotta ask you two to call it a night. Maybe you don't need sleep, but the rest of us do."

While Nola went to the restroom, Mason signed away several days' pay on his credit card. The bartender yawned as he unlocked the door for them to leave.

"We closed the place down," Mason said as he opened Nola's car door. "High-school teachers don't do that too often."

"I *never* do that." She stifled a yawn of her own. "I get up and go to bed early."

"I like sleeping late." Mason braced his forearm on the passenger seat as he turned to look through the rear window while backing out. With the car again in gear, his right hand strayed to capture Nola's once more. She curled her fingers around his.

They didn't speak on the drive back to city hall, or on the walk from his car to hers. When Nola unlocked her door and turned, she found Mason standing very close, barely a breath away.

She didn't step back. "Thank you so much. I haven't had such a lovely dinner since…well, maybe never."

"Even though I tricked you into it?"

"Even though you tricked me into it."

They gazed at each other for a long moment. Then Mason looked up. "You parked in the shadiest corner of this lot."

Nola made a show of consulting her watch. "It's after midnight. We don't worry about shade between midnight and dawn."

"True." His hands bridged the distance between them by closing over her shoulders. "But the trees that give daytime shade also screen us from the road in the dark. So nobody passing by will notice when I do this." He pulled her up against him. His hands slid slowly down her back.

"Or this…" His teeth closed gently on her lower lip, played a little, then released. She took a quick breath, and he repeated the caress with her upper lip. As Nola returned the favor, Mason grasped her hips. Slipping her hands under his jacket, she shaped the lines of his body through the soft shirt he wore. "You feel so *good*," she whispered.

The kisses got crazy after that, hot and hard. She dragged his shirt out of his slacks, and her palms caressed his back, his ribs. His buttons slipped free without either of them trying, baring his chest to her mouth. Mason's hips pressed her against the car, with his hands hot on her skin, pushing away her bra, covering her breasts, fingering the peaks. She moved against him and he groaned, bending his knees to lift her slightly off her feet, stroking a hand over her thigh.

A bright light flashed in Mason's face. A deep voice with a hillbilly twang said, "What you folks up to here?"

He lifted his head and stared across the roof of the school car at a Ridgeville policeman. "Exactly what it looks like, Officer."

"Hmm." The light flashed over the car door, where the Hawkridge seal was discreetly emblazoned. "Kinda late to be out in town, ain't it?"

"Yes, it is." Back on her own feet, Nola shuddered against

him, with laughter or horror, Mason didn't know which. "If you'll give us two minutes, we'll be gone."

For a moment, he wasn't sure the officer would agree. He feared he'd be called upon to step away from the car with his hands up, which would expose his unbuttoned shirt and his fading but still obvious arousal. Would they end up in jail? What a mess that would be.

But then darkness masked them as the light clicked off. "Y'all got three minutes to exit the premises." Gravel crunched as the policeman walked back to his car, parked only yards away. Mason couldn't believe they hadn't heard it approach.

Then again, given Nola's effect on him, maybe he could. He backed up, buttoning haphazardly. "Are you okay?"

She was still nearly speechless—with laughter, he was glad to see. "I've never been caught necking before." She wiped her eyes with her fingers. "Another first."

He wanted to make some meaningful romantic gesture, but the moment seemed to have passed. How to phrase the invitation? "You could—" he started.

Beside them, the police-car engine revved. "You folks get on your way, now," the officer called through his open window.

Mason sent a wave in the officer's direction, squeezed Nola's arm gently and headed off to his own vehicle. What a way to end an evening.

Nola's headlights followed him out of town and along the twisting road leading back to school. He thought about pulling over to the side—she would stop, and he could invite her to come home with him then.

Even if the shoulders of the road hadn't been too narrow for parking, however, the set of headlights behind Nola's car discouraged any delays. The damn cop followed them all the way to the Hawkridge gates.

Luckily, only one set of lights pursued him along the school road. Mason had cooled down enough to realize how outrageous his behavior had been, and didn't consider pulling over on the grass to ask Nola to spend the night with him. Surely she knew that was what he wanted. He took the small side road leading directly to the hunting lodge. She would follow, of course. He couldn't mistake her response. She wanted him as much as he wanted her.

He used his turn signal so she would understand his intention. He made the turn, slowly, carefully.

Then braked and sat staring through the rearview mirror in astonishment as Nola drove straight past the side road, heading for the Manor and the faculty parking lot.

She'd turned him down.

IN THE BATHROOM of Pink's Cottage, Nola stared at the woman in the mirror, lightly fingering the redness around her mouth left by Mason's kisses. He'd raked his fingers through her hair over and over again, dragged his mouth and teeth along her throat. She leaned closer and tilted her head to the left, exposing her neck to the light. Dear God, Mason had left a— a hickey on her neck!

Heart pounding, she stripped off her clothes, threw on a nightgown and crawled under the covers. Alone. She'd thought about following him home, turning onto that small road in his wake and ending up at the lodge, in Mason's room. In his bed.

But common sense had intruded just in time, preventing her from making a terrible mistake. If someone saw the car she'd borrowed parked in front of the lodge, the whole campus would know within hours that she'd slept with Mason. She could only imagine the complications that would create with students and faculty. The prospect terrified her.

Even worse, what if they did make love, and she disappointed him? Her other lovers had never been terribly impressed. One of them had called her frigid. The idea that she might leave Mason unsatisfied paralyzed her.

A thought struck her then, hard enough to drive the breath from her lungs. She'd never once worried about satisfying Ted. His kisses were, well, warm, and she'd expected sex between them to be okay. Had she really been prepared to be happy with okay sex for the rest of her life?

Nothing about Mason was merely okay. He set her on fire whenever, wherever he touched her. His kisses made her ache, made her crave. Made her desperate to give.

But she'd been in this vulnerable place before—at the age of eighteen. In the years since, she'd been careful to remember the lesson Mason taught her. Never depend upon desire.

And yet she surrendered to the physical storm he woke in her at the least provocation. She was afraid she knew the reason Mason stirred her as no man ever had. If she admitted she loved him, would that improve the situation—or only make it worse?

She fell asleep with the question still unanswered, just as she heard birds begin to chirp outside her open window. Only minutes later, it seemed, she was awake again. The dull ringing in her ears turned out to be the telephone.

"Nola? Are you okay?" Mason sounded as if he was standing in the doorway.

She sat straight up in bed. "Um, yes. Yes, I'm fine. What's wrong?"

"You haven't been outside?"

A squint at the clock told her she'd slept until noon. "No." The urgency in his voice finally reached her. "What's wrong?"

"There's been another episode of vandalism—graffiti on the walls of the Manor itself. Everybody's in an uproar, but I didn't see you in the crowd."

"What kind of graffiti? What did it say?"

"Various unflattering characterizations of the girls at Hawkridge."

She sat up in bed, pushing her hair out of her eyes. "We're both adults, Mason. I can take the unvarnished truth."

"'Slut' was the least offensive term," he said, sounding embarrassed. "And that's as specific as I'll get."

Nola could fill in the blanks for herself. "Are the girls upset?"

"Most of them are laughing, or pretending to. Tommy's called a meeting in the gym for two o'clock, faculty included."

"I'll see you then," she promised and hung up, still avoiding his question.

She got a chance to view the damage herself on the way to the meeting—ugly words scrawled in black paint across the old rose brick and soft gray stone of the Manor. Girls gathered in knots of two and three, some grave and silent, some loudly indignant, some defiant and amused.

Zara stood alone, one shoulder propped against a lamppost. Nola hoped their meeting appeared casual, though she'd intended all along to seek out the girl.

She didn't waste time on greetings. "You're the one wandering the campus at all hours. Did you do this?"

"No." Zara's expression gave nothing away.

"Did you see anyone else on the grounds last night?"

She chuckled. "Just you. Late night, huh?"

Nola hadn't been aware of being watched. "What are you suggesting?" she demanded, staring at Zara until she dropped her gaze to her boots.

"Nothing."

Beyond them, Ruth Ann came striding down the walk. "Can you believe this? It has to be someone from town. None of our girls would make this sort of mess."

Zara faded into the landscape of girls while Nola went into the gymnasium with Ruth Ann. All the teachers sat among the students, as a gesture of solidarity.

Jayne Thomas came in accompanied by a police officer whose dark blue uniform reminded Nola all too forcibly of the night before. Her gaze wandered to Mason, sitting at the other end of the bleachers, and she found him looking back at her. She felt her face flush. Underneath her turtleneck, the bruise on her throat throbbed.

"We have a problem," the headmistress said when the crowd settled down. "On five separate occasions, the integrity of the Hawkridge facility has been violated." She waited until the girls' reaction had subsided again. "First, a dead animal was left on the front steps of the school."

"It was a skunk," the girl on Nola's right whispered to her neighbor. "Stank to high heaven!"

"Then windows were broken in the dormitory and library over spring break. Two days later, the pillars of the front gates and the Hawkridge School sign were coated with paint."

"Brown paint," the same girl said. "Looked like a giant baby had pooped all over them." The students around Nola started to giggle, and she got them quiet just as Jayne Thomas flashed an irritated glance in their direction.

"The school's cars and vans have been damaged. Today, for the first time, the vandal threatened our students directly, and that is the most serious violation of all. Neither I, nor the faculty, nor the board of directors will tolerate such insults to our girls."

She leaned forward, bracing her arms on the speaker's stand. "If anyone here has any information that could lead us to the person committing these crimes—yes, these are criminal acts—I plead with you to give us that information. The mind behind such damage could become more dangerous and threaten any of you individually. Please, if you know something, tell me—or tell a teacher you trust. We want to stop this before somebody gets hurt.

"To that end, Police Chief Clement would like to talk to you for a few minutes."

The chief said all the official and appropriate words about

staying safe and reporting unusual activity or strangers on campus. Then Sam Malcolm, the security chief for Hawkridge, echoed the chief's comments and pointed out places on campus where girls should not go alone, including Hawk's Ridge.

"These days," he said, "you can't be too careful."

"Maybe it's a terrorist," one student said. "The next step might be a bomb!"

Even as hysteria swelled among the girls, Jayne Thomas took the microphone from its stand. "This is not a terrorist," she said, and her words bounced off the gym walls. "This is someone with a grudge against our school, playing pranks to make us mad. Getting upset will make this person happy. Our best revenge is to continue as we've always done—classes, meals and extracurricular activities will proceed as usual. The spring dance is coming up, and even before that, the annual May Day celebration. Stay calm, be careful, and we'll have another beautiful spring to remember at Hawkridge School."

The girls dispersed quickly—except for the one who'd suggested terrorism, who was being walked toward the headmistress with Alice Tolbert's new rainbow-striped nails around her arm.

Nola stayed seated as the gym emptied. She wanted to believe Zara's denial, but didn't know if she could. What kind of evidence might prove the girl's innocence? Or guilt?

"Those are deep thoughts—they must be worth all of a dollar."

She jumped as Mason spoke directly in front of her. "Ten at least." Ignoring the hand he extended, she stood and side-stepped to the stairs so she could leave the bleachers.

By the time she reached the floor, he had pulled a ten-dollar bill from his wallet. "So, spill them."

Shaking her head, she continued toward the exit. "I've decided on an auction. My thoughts go to the highest bidder."

Mason stopped and watched her walk away. The highest bidder, indeed. What would it take to win Nola Shannon's trust?

She would want everything a man had to give, he thought, heart and soul, mind and body. Did he have it in him to offer? Could he face the rest of his life if he let her go again?

Chapter Twelve

The Hawkridge May Day tradition was a remnant of th Ridgely pretensions to an aristocratic British heritage. Agath Ridgely had stipulated the celebration in her will establish ing Hawkridge as a school for girls of "good families" wh stood in need of "extra guidance."

Each year, a maypole decked with brightly colored ribbon appeared on the Hawkridge lawn—though this was the fir year a sentry had stood watch all night to prevent an mischief. At noon, there would be a picnic for faculty, sta and students, a dance around the maypole, songs and game Classes were suspended for the day and uniforms wer replaced by white dresses. No one had ever flouted that pa ticular rule, and Nola wondered if Zara would be the first.

She, herself, had to be the first person awake on this pa ticular May Day. Her brain had started working at 4:00 a.m and would not shut down. So she'd taken her shower an made coffee. Now dressed in a warm robe, she was sitting i bed, working on her research, although not at all succes fully. Though her brain didn't want to go back to sleep, didn't seem interested in pursuing a mathematical line of re soning, either.

Which might have been why she heard the noise—th

scrape of a metal chair on the stone terrace, a rattle at the back door. She thought first of a wild animal, or that even one of Garrett's menagerie had escaped to track her down.

Her second thought, however, zeroed in on the vandal plaguing the school. Perhaps they thought Pink's Cottage was unoccupied and planned to wreck the place.

Boy, would they be surprised. Moving silently through the dark house, Nola went to the kitchen and picked up the cast-iron frying pan she'd set out for this morning's omelet. Wielded like a baseball bat, it would make an effective weapon.

At the door, she released the chain and the lock without making a sound. Then, with a quick turn of her wrist, she flung it open, grabbing the frying pan with both hands in preparation for her swing.

Mason stared back at her from the darkness on the other side of the threshold.

"Good God, don't hit me! I've got a young son to raise."

She lowered the frying pan. "And where is he while you're prowling around at 4:00 a.m.?"

"At home, asleep."

"Alone?"

"Gail's parents are visiting, as you know. He's perfectly safe." He lifted his hands, which cradled a small basket filled with flowers. "It's May Day. I was leaving you a token."

Nola found her voice. "Before dawn?"

"I know you get up early. I didn't want to get caught."

She took the basket from him and was immediately enveloped by a rich perfume. "Oh, Mason. Hyacinths. How wonderful!"

He tilted his head and smiled. "The blue reminded me of your eyes."

That statement left her speechless. She'd done a good job of avoiding him these past two weeks, meeting with Zara at

Pink's Cottage, slipping away from volleyball games as soon as the final point was scored. It helped that he'd been out of town several times, attending conferences in different parts of the country.

One more month and she might just escape from Hawkridge intact.

"What are you doing up at this hour, anyway?" he asked. "Is this what you mean by early? My term would be 'uncivilized.'"

Nola found her voice. "I couldn't sleep. I thought I'd try working."

Lifting his chin, he sniffed the air. "Is that coffee? Real coffee?"

The next move was obvious. "Come in and have some." With the hyacinth basket centered on the kitchen table, she returned the frying pan to its place, took a mug from the cupboard and filled it to the brim. "Black, is that right?"

Mason took the cup and sipped. "Perfect. I usually make do with instant."

Nola poured herself another mug, adding cream and sugar. "Have you heard of this amazing invention, the automatic coffeemaker? They even come with timers, so you can set them up the night before and have your coffee ready exactly when you want it in the morning."

He shook his head. "Too much trouble."

She gazed at him over the rim of her cup. "You don't take care of yourself."

"Sure I do. Dentist twice a year, doctor once in a while." He shrugged. "I'm fine."

"Yes, but…" This was dangerous territory. Nola stared into her coffee for a moment, wondering if she had the courage to proceed. "But you don't seem to allow yourself the pleasures of life."

Mason set his cup on the counter. "Pleasures?"

"You teach the girls and you take care of Garrett. You love

food, but you don't cook much. You love good coffee, but settle for instant." She took a fortifying sip of her own. "You don't design airplanes anymore, or play sports. You read about movies, but don't go unless Garrett can go, too. You're just watching life pass by, Mason. That's not like you."

He didn't say anything for a long time, but stood with his head bowed, his arms crossed over his chest, leaning against the edge of the counter with his ankles crossed. A gray sweatshirt hung loose on his shoulders. Gray sweatpants draped the muscles of his legs. His hair was messy, maybe even uncombed. Nola ached to run her fingers through it.

Finally, he looked at her, one eyebrow lifted quizzically. "I'm a little confused, being instructed on the pleasures of life by a woman who lives for nothing but her work, which is theoretical mathematics. Not the most sensual of topics." He looked her up and down. "You've lost weight," he added. "So much for the pleasure of food."

She realized she'd finished her coffee and she set the mug down. "I'm aware of the irony."

"But I can see your point," he said. "It's just… When Gail…" He shook his head.

"You've had a really hard time." Nola stepped close enough to put her hand on his wrist where the sweatshirt sleeve fell back. "No one can be the same after losing the wife he loved."

His eyes smiled into hers. "You've had your own hard breaks. I guess we're two of a kind." He slipped his arm backward, and turned his hand to link his thumb with hers. The slide of skin against skin, the impact of bone on bone, went through her like an electric shock.

"When you're—what's a good word, *deprived?*—of something or someone vital," Mason said, "maybe you try to avoid other pleasures in your life because feeling even a small pleasure reminds you of everything you've lost." He slipped his hand free, but only to stroke his palm along her forearm. Then he cupped her elbow and brought her closer.

"I miss having someone to hold," he said in a low voice. "I've been lying in bed alone for most of the last three years, feeling like the world is completely empty. Wishing I could just crumble into dust, myself. If it weren't for Garrett, I don't know what I would have done."

"Mason!" She pressed her palm to his chest, over his heart. "No."

He lifted one shoulder. "Luckily, Garrett needed me. Kids get you up every morning and keep you going all day until you fall into bed, even if you can't sleep."

He touched his forehead to hers. "Then you arrived." That roughness was back in his voice, a dark current threading through every word. "I don't lie in the empty darkness anymore. I lie awake thinking about you." His arm came around her and pulled her hard against him. "Wanting you."

"Mason—" But it was only a token protest.

And he knew it. "Maybe we should explore those pleasures we're missing," he murmured against her lips. "Together."

They played with kisses for quite a while, testing the fit of mouth against mouth, the brush of soft flesh over even softer, the contrasts of taste in bitter and sweet. Nola slipped her hand up to cup the nape of his neck, to finger his hair over his ears. Moments later, the sash of her robe dropped away and Mason's palm curved against her waist. She gasped at his touch.

"Mmm," he growled deep in his chest. He pulled back a little, to see what he'd revealed. The fleece robe clung to her shoulders and covered her arms, but little else. She was thin and small but… "Beautiful," Mason whispered, and saw the flush rise from her breastbone.

Then he noticed the green shadow of the bruise on her throat. "Did I do that?" He touched the mark with his fingers as she nodded. "Should I apologize?"

Nola shook her head, and he grinned. "I'll try to be more…um…discreet."

She smiled back at him. "Thanks."

He bent to kiss the bruise, and then brushed his tongue over it. Nola gasped and clutched at his shoulders, and together they went wild.

When her knees buckled, he carried her to the bedroom, leaving the robe and his sweatshirt behind them on the floor of the kitchen. A notebook of wild scribbling lay open on the bed. Mason laid Nola in the place where she'd obviously slept and then carefully moved her work to a nearby chest.

When he turned back she'd taken off her panties and lay naked, waiting for him. He put a hand on his chest. "You should have warned me. The sight of you is enough to give a man a heart attack."

She didn't laugh. "I might disappoint you."

Holding her gaze, he toed off his sneakers, got rid of his sweatpants. "Not possible. You're Nola, and that's all I need." Pulling back the pristine white bedspread, he lay down beside her. "Love me, Nola. That's all I want."

She came to him in a rush, skin against smooth, glorious skin. After only seconds, he couldn't tell where he ended and she began—they were just one delirious, passionate creature, angles and curves, hills and hollows, rough but smooth, soft yet hard. Moving together, then apart, they trembled, ached, soared and finally ignited.

"Afterglow." Mason chuckled, when he could get enough breath. "They should call it afterburn." He bent to kiss Nola's head where it rested on his chest. "You burned me up, woman."

Her "Mmm" rumbled through him, but she didn't move.

"Are you going to sleep on me?" He ran his fingers down the curve of her spine, marveling at the freedom to do so.

"Lit'rally," she mumbled.

He closed his eyes in contentment. "Be my guest."

* * *

NOLA AWOKE ALONE, with a bar of sunlight across her eyes. A squint at the clock told her she should be grateful classes were canceled, since she'd missed first *and* second periods. With a luxurious sigh, she burrowed into the hollow in her pillow left by Mason's head and fell back asleep.

The phone roused her a second time. Expecting Mason, she rolled over and answered with a sleepy, "Mmm?"

"Nola? Nola, it's Ted."

That woke her up fast. "Ted." Oh, God. She couldn't… "Hi, Ted. How are you?"

He spent several minutes describing the bout of flu he'd just suffered through. "Four days later, the fever came back and I was coughing so hard I bruised my rib muscles."

"Many of the girls here have had the same virus." She rubbed her eyes and scratched her head, trying to wake up properly. "You'll feel better soon."

"I hope so. I'm still in bed, though—I got my teaching assistant to handle my classes for the day. That's why I can call in the middle of the morning."

He didn't sound that sick. "I can't talk too long," she told him. "The May Day ceremony starts in an hour."

"How perfectly archaic," Ted said. "You have a maypole and everything?"

"It's a Hawkridge tradition." Nola sat up and slipped her feet to the floor. "In fact, I'd better get going. I forgot, but I'm supposed to help set up the refreshment tables."

"Do they have any idea who you are? They have a prize-winning Ph.D. teaching high schoolers, and on top of it all they want you to do janitorial work?"

"I'm glad to hear from you," Nola lied. "I'll call on the weekend." She hung up without waiting for Ted to say goodbye.

She would have to break off with him, of course. Maybe there hadn't been anything definite between them, but she couldn't make love to one man while planning a life with someone else.

Once again, Mason Reed had crushed her hopes for a lasting, meaningful relationship.

AS IT ALWAYS DID, the Hawkridge School May Day celebration proceeded flawlessly. More than a few of the adults blinked hard or wiped their cheeks while listening to the lovely rise and fall of young women's voices in the mountain air. For once, the local dignitaries invited for the occasion didn't talk too long, and Jayne was witty but brief, as always. The maypole dance drew laughter, and the picnic afterward showcased the full range of Mrs. Werner's talents.

Mason stood with his hands in the pockets of his linen trousers, watching the students, all dressed in white, enjoying their lunch in the meadow, while Garrett blew bubbles into the breeze and, on either side of him, Gail's parents tried to talk him out of continuing his job search.

"What would you do," Myra Chance asked, "if Garrett got sick and needed care? You'd have no one nearby to look after him."

"I've handled that before," he reminded her with as much patience as he could muster. "He had the flu last month and we managed." Right now, he was the one with the headache. From lack of sleep.

At the thought, he barely kept the grin off his face.

"The boy loves the farm," Gail's father said. "He's getting along real well learning to ride Gail's pony. Why take him away from his mother's roots?"

"I expect we'd see you as often as we do now." Mason took a deep breath. "I have a pilot's license, remember? And a plane. Even from Washington state, we could easily fly out and spend the weekend."

"I don't think—" Myra started.

But Mason had caught sight of Garrett, who had Nola by the hand and was leading her toward them while also talking a mile a minute. He closed his eyes for a second in sheer relief. He'd needed to see her since the moment he'd stepped out of her door and into the chilly morning.

She looked slender and gorgeous in a simple white linen dress that skimmed her curves from shoulders to hips and swirled around her ankles. A wide-brimmed straw hat framed her face.

He wanted to kiss her hello. But aside from the circumstances of this meeting, there was a wariness in her face that warned him off.

So he tempered the warmth of his greeting. "Nola Shannon, I'd like you to meet Garrett's grandparents, Dale and Myra Chance. Nola," he explained to Myra, "has stepped in for one of our teachers on maternity leave this spring."

"Good to meet you, Nola." Dale Chance extended a weathered farmer's hand to shake hers.

Myra nodded—curtly, Mason thought. "Hello." She gave Nola the once-over. "What do you teach?"

"Math," Nola said.

Dale shook his head. "That's a hard one. I was never real good at math."

"Nola's on leave from her regular position," Mason explained. "She's a professor at an Ivy League college in Boston and does high-level research in mathematics. She was also a student at Hawkridge when I started teaching here."

Gail's mother lifted her chin. "Really? You started dating Gail soon after you arrived in town, didn't you, Mason?"

"Yes, I did." As if he needed reminding.

Myra sniffed and turned toward Garrett. "I think I'd like some more lemonade. Garrett, will you come with me?"

Garrett glanced at Mason, who nodded. "Sure," Garrett said. "I mean, yes, ma'am." With his grandmother holding his hand, he walked off toward the food tent.

The atmosphere eased with Myra's departure. Nola asked Dale about his farm and what he produced, which earned her an extended explanation of profit-loss ratios on corn and melon crops.

"It seems to me you do quite a bit of math," she told him, "in order to make your farm profitable."

"Oh, that's just adding and subtracting, with a little multiplication thrown in."

"I'd be lost, trying to get seeds into the ground at the right time and knowing exactly when to harvest."

The older man shrugged. "Common sense, that's all."

She glanced at Mason, smiling, and a spark of what they'd shared this morning shot through him. "Common sense is something we mathematicians are notoriously lacking."

They were still sharing that smile when Jayne Thomas joined them. She greeted Dale politely, but then turned to Mason. "We've had another incident," she said in a low voice. "Can you and Nola come with me?"

After excusing themselves they strolled across the grass without urgency—Jayne wanted to attract as little attention as possible. "No sense spoiling the party." They entered the Manor by the east door. Once inside, her pace increased abruptly.

"What's happened?" Mason stepped ahead to open the door into the main hall. "What have they done? Oh, God."

Nola, standing just behind Jayne, gasped. Red paint flowed down the curved staircase, dripping from step to step, a grotesque stain on the white marble. The same paint had been flung against the mahogany-paneled walls and dashed across the black-and-white floor.

"It looks like blood," Nola whispered.

"I'm sure that's intentional." Jayne cleared her throat. "I'd say it's a definite threat."

"I'd say the same." Chief Clement stood at the open front door, making notes. "And I'd say you've only got one option."

Jayne's shoulders stiffened. "And that is?"

"Close this place down."

Closing down was not an option Tommy would consider, of course. A superficial cleanup was completed before dinner, though the old stone and wood of the entry hall still bore traces of the assault. The girls discovered what had happened soon enough, and talk at dinner revolved around plans for catching the vandal and enacting a suitable revenge.

The police had nothing better to offer. No one had noticed a stranger wandering around, other than the florist and his assistants, invited guests and extra workers hired to help with tables and chairs.

"This person is crazy smart," Mason said late Sunday afternoon as he stood with Nola watching an impromptu student soccer game. "We'll have to be crazy to catch him. Or her."

"Means, motive, opportunity—isn't that what TV detectives look for?" Nola sighed. "Someone comes onto campus undetected, makes a mess for a reason we don't understand and then escapes. Not very promising."

He turned his back to the game and stared at the mountains instead. "How are you?"

Nola watched the girls race toward one end of the field. "I'm fine. Shouldn't you be at home?"

"I came out for a walk. Dale and Myra are good people, but losing Gail was a hard blow and they haven't recovered. Still, I can only handle so much 'remember when...'"

She lifted a hand toward him, but then let it fall before she touched him. "Of course."

"Myra was awake the other morning when I got back to the house." Mason pivoted to watch the game again. "I told her I'd been running."

"Did she believe you?"

"She had no reason not to. And no business caring one way or the other." He glanced around, then moved a step closer. "I thought I might go running again tomorrow morning. What do you think?" He held his breath, not sure what she would say.

She gave him a slow, sexy smile. "Oh, I definitely think you need the exercise."

SUNDAY NIGHT, Nola called Ted. "I'm sorry I had to rush off the phone the other morning. I really did have to hurry."

"No problem." He sounded rested, unhurried. "How's it going down there in Dogpatch?"

His reference to an old comic strip strengthened her resolve. "Ted, listen, I want you to know that things will be different when I get back to Boston."

"Different how? Are you taking on another class? I thought you needed more time for research."

"This isn't about work. I mean things…between us… will change."

"Explain?"

Nola took a deep breath. "I'll always be your friend, but our relationship won't be going any further."

After a moment, she heard him sigh. "I'm sorry about that. I thought we would make a compatible couple. Good partners for the long haul."

Now, she felt like a monster. "I did, too. But my feelings became clear once I got some space and a chance to think. We shouldn't settle for 'compatible,' Ted. There's more to a relationship that just being comfortable."

"Sounds like you've found your soul mate."

Possibly. Probably. "I don't know. I only know that you should look for someone who makes you deliriously happy. It's worth the wait."

"Right." He sighed again. "Thanks for letting me know. And tell the lucky bastard congratulations from me."

Chapter Thirteen

"Any more questions?" Nola turned from the board to survey her Friday-morning fourth-period class. A few of them shook their heads. Coupled with the many hands raised during class, she felt as if they'd made real progress since that first awful day in March.

"The test will begin as soon as the bell rings on Monday. Arrive promptly, so you'll be ready." With perfect timing, the lunch bell rang at that moment, and her students rushed away.

Nola erased her board carefully, preparing for the next class. She picked up the brown grocery bag hiding under her desk, looked longingly at the chair where she lunched every day, then propelled herself through the classroom door into the main hall, up staircase steps still tinged with red and into the teachers' lounge on the second floor.

"Hey, there." Alice Tolbert greeted her just inside. "We've got all the food here on the table. As soon as everybody arrives—everybody but Mason, since he's off gallivanting somewhere—we'll eat."

This was the annual potluck luncheon the teachers gave themselves every year in May, after the madness of May Day but before the spring dance and the insanity of exams and graduation. Nola had hesitated to attend, since she hadn't spent much time in the teachers' lounge since her arrival, but Alice had taken for granted that she'd be coming and ordered her to bring a fruit salad. Now, with a big bowl of fresh local strawberries in hand, she'd arrived.

To her surprise she enjoyed herself very much indeed. The food was wonderful, from Ruth Ann's fried chicken to the French teacher's plate of cheeses to Alice's decadent fudge brownies. Nola found herself laughing, eating more than she usually consumed in an entire day, and actually talking while she ate.

"Mason would have brought packaged cookies," Ruth Ann commented as they cleaned up together after the meal. "The man has been hopeless about food since Gail got sick. Lord only knows what he and Garrett eat for dinner most nights."

Nola had the presence of mind to conceal what she knew about that issue. "I imagine he hadn't yet learned to cook when he and Gail married and she just took on the task, so he never tried."

"I guess. Gail certainly took good care of him. We all wondered if he'd make it by himself." She sent Nola a sideways glance. "He did make it, barely. Lately, though, I've noticed he's perking up. Playing volleyball, even running in the mornings. Our plan is working."

"You've seen him running?" Nola's heart plunged to the pit of her stomach. She bent to tie the top of the trash bag, hoping to hide her face.

"I'm up with the horses by five-thirty most mornings. I've noticed him jogging toward the lodge a couple of times recently." When Nola looked up again, Ruth Ann winked at her. "I think it's great. He needs that kind of, um, exercise."

Before Nola could think of what to say, the fifth-period warning bell rang. "Gotta go." Ruth Ann gave her a backward wave as she went through the door. "Thanks for the help!"

With three more classes to review for Monday's tests, Nola

had little time to reflect on that conversation until the end of the day. But as she packed up her books and papers, she concluded that she'd received Ruth Ann's approval for a relationship with Mason. Perhaps the other teachers—even Jayne Thomas—would agree.

Walking slowly through the cool mist for which the Smoky Mountains were famous, Nola considered the possibility. Loving Mason went without saying. She'd loved him for twelve years, and had finally stopped denying the truth to herself.

Still, a commitment to Mason, assuming he wanted one, would demand huge changes. He and Garrett might come to Boston. Mason could teach high school anywhere. But she had a feeling Garrett would hate her sixteenth-floor apartment, the cityscape of concrete stretching miles in every direction. They could buy property at the beach or in the Berkshire mountains. Would the little boy ever consider that home?

Moving her life to North Carolina would create its own problems. Hawkridge provided a lovely retreat from the demands and tensions of her professional life. But Nola had made a place for herself on a wider stage. Her research could continue across the Internet, of course, with frequent trips to university centers. She enjoyed the collegial atmosphere, however, the stimulation of several minds attacking the same problem. Teaching high-school algebra, even to girls as challenging as Zara, lacked the excitement of a graduate seminar in fractal theory. Diversity, cutting-edge science, theater and music, art and food... She would undoubtedly miss that world.

Yet she loved being with Mason, and with Garrett. They might be her one chance to have a family. She could never share with anyone else what she'd given wholeheartedly to Mason Reed.

So intense were her thoughts that she didn't realize she'd walked right past Pink's Cottage until she heard Garrett's voice.

"Ms. Shannon? Hey, Ms. Shannon!"

She saw him running toward her out of the trees. "Hi, Garrett. What's going on?"

He stopped just short of knocking into her, grabbed her free hand and started back the way he'd come, pulling her along. "I need your help. Please, they really need us."

She followed, but asked, "Who? Is something wrong with your grandparents?"

He shook his head, tugging harder, trying to go faster. "Not them. The kittens. I checked this morning and the mother wasn't there, so I figured she was out hunting. I don't think she's been back, though, and they're starving to death!"

"Kittens?" She slowed down, tried to stop. "Garrett, maybe—"

But he resisted her effort with a strength that surprised her. "Come on!"

Once inside the forest Garrett led her off the path and through the underbrush. Her shoes disappeared under pine needles and fallen leaves, where the ground dipped suddenly. Fallen trees had to be scrambled over rather than walked around. Nola couldn't believe Garrett knew where he was going in this wilderness. She wondered if he could get them back to the lodge before dark.

All at once, he stopped, turned and put a finger to his lips for silence. "Maybe she's back," he whispered. "I don't hear them."

Nola looked around. The only place kittens could be hiding was in the huge hollow log just ahead. Like Garrett, though, she didn't hear any kitten sounds.

She stood still as he crept toward the log, making no sound. Kneeling at one end, he leaned over to look inside. Then, just as quietly, he stood up, turned and came back to her side.

"She's there," he said in a low voice, with a grin very much like his dad's. "All curled up, feeding them. Whew!" He pretended to wipe sweat off his forehead. "Grandma would have hated me bringing home six kittens." He looked at her out of the corners of his eyes. "I would have had to give them to you."

Nola laughed. "You would have had to come to the cottage and take care of them yourself. I wouldn't have a clue what to do with six kittens."

They walked back the way they'd come at a more reasonable pace. This time, Garrett allowed Nola to go around fallen trees rather than over them.

As they approached the edge of the forest, though, he glanced up at the treetops high above them. "Ms. Shannon, do you believe in heaven?"

She followed his gaze. Was this a test? How should she answer? "Um, I think there's a life after this one, though I'm not sure exactly what that means."

When she looked at Garrett, he was gazing back at her. "Do you think people in that life can talk to people in this one?"

"Like ghosts?" She had a feeling she was flunking the exam.

He shook his head, then brushed back the dark hair in his eyes with grubby fingers. "No, just…well, maybe somebody here needs help. Do you think somebody from over there could tell them what to do?"

His mother, in other words. As they reached the head of the path and the edge of the Manor lawn, Nola stopped. "I've never had that happen," she said gently. "But here's what I think. If you love somebody very much, you always carry them in your heart. What they would think, what they would do, becomes a part of the way you think and act." She took a deep breath. "So maybe, when you're figuring things out, you remember what that person would say. And it's like they've talked to you about it."

Garrett stared up at her as she spoke, his face solemn, his hazel eyes focused intently. "Maybe." He looked down at his feet for a moment. "Maybe."

Then, without warning, he threw his arms around her waist.

"Thanks, Ms. Shannon." His hug was strong. Powerful. "For everything."

In the next instant, he went running off—not along the path toward the lodge, but through the woods on some unseen trail of his own.

Nola stood motionless for a moment. Then she walked back to Pink's Cottage, blinking against tears all the way home.

LATE SATURDAY AFTERNOON, Mason climbed wearily from his car and pulled his bag from the backseat. If the world were perfect, he could have said hello to his son, downed a tall glass of water, then stretched out on the sofa with his shoes off and his head in Nola's lap.

But the world wasn't perfect. When he stepped into the kitchen, both Dale and Myra glared at him from the kitchen table.

"I'm home," he announced. "Did everything go all right?"

"Garrett's fine." Myra nodded toward the windows. "He's out back with the animals."

Mason went to the sink and ran that glass of water he'd been needing for the last two hours. After gulping half of it, he turned around. "I really appreciate you both being here to take care of him. I don't worry when I know he's in such capable hands."

No response.

He sighed. "And I'm sorry about the argument we had before I left." He took another gulp, remembering the speech he'd practiced while in Illinois. "But I'm a grown man with the right to a private life. I loved your daughter with all my heart. I did everything I could to take care of her. She's gone now, but I'm not. Do you really expect me to stop living?"

Dale glanced uneasily at his wife. "I think you owe respect to her memory."

"I will always have the greatest respect for Gail's memory."

Myra bristled. "Sneaking out at night is not respectful!"

Mason squeezed his eyes shut for a second. "The situation is unusual. If Nola and I were living in a regular community, this wouldn't be an issue."

He dragged in a deep breath. "Either way, I don't see my relationship with Nola as disrespectful. Gail taught me so much about love, and now I'm sharing what I've learned with…" He let his voice trail off.

Yes, indeed. He loved Nola Shannon.

The back door slammed, and footsteps pounded up the steps. "Dad! Dad, you're home!" Garrett's head hit him in the solar plexus, while two arms and two legs wrapped tight around him.

Grinning, Mason bent over to hug his son. "Good to see you, too. What's going on?"

Once Garrett started talking there was no stopping him, and Mason was glad to be distracted, to be taken down to see the animals, to hear the story about Nola and the kittens. He helped with the feeding and cleaning, settling back into a routine he knew would never be quite the same again.

He'd fallen in love with Nola Shannon. All the way this time. There could be no going back, no pretending it hadn't happened.

But at this point, he wasn't in the least certain he could see any way for the two of them—three, counting Garrett—to make a future together.

And wasn't that a hell of a mess?

HAVING BEEN KICKED out of two different schools for cheating, Nola took a proactive approach to tests. She spent Monday walking the aisles between the tables in her classroom while her students worked. After a long, quiet day, the volleyball game—especially with Mason on the other team—gave her a chance to blow off steam. She made herself eat dinner and clean up the kitchen. Finally, she sat down to grade the day's tests. Now she would discover if their work with Zara had succeeded.

Still, she postponed the most important moment by grading all the first-period tests and recording the scores, rather than skipping immediately to Zara's. Refusing to give in to her curiosity, she worked on the second-period tests in the order in which they'd been turned in. Zara's was one of the last to be graded.

Then she called Mason.

"Hey," he said in that rich, warm drawl of his. "I'm sorry I didn't get a chance to say hello during classes today. My every move is being watched."

"I'm sure."

"So how are you?"

"Pretty devastated, actually."

"What's wrong?"

She could hardly bring herself to say the words. "Zara failed today's test."

Wednesday's news was just as bad—Zara had also failed her physics test. Mason reported the results to Jayne Thomas before lunch, and the four of them met in her office at three-thirty that afternoon.

Jayne gazed at Zara for a minute in silence. "These scores aren't what we'd hoped for," she said. "Have you got an explanation, Zara? A reason you did poorly on your tests?"

Zara answered with the standard shrug, keeping her face turned toward the office window.

"I'm afraid that's not acceptable. Give me something to work with, Zara. Give me a reason to help you."

After a long silence, Nola said, "Zara told me last week that she gets nervous before tests, and that makes it hard to think."

"Test anxiety." Jayne nodded. "We can work on that. Is there something else going on, Zara? A personal problem we can help you with?"

"No," she mumbled. "Everything's cool."

"Well, this is the same song, tenth verse. You have to pass

these courses to graduate. Your improved homework and quiz grades have brought your average in both classes close to that possibility. Fortunately, the tests didn't eliminate your chances, though they didn't help as we'd hoped they would. Your final exams will be the deciding factor. You'll need at least an eighty percent on both math and physics in order to graduate."

Jayne waited for a comment and Zara finally sighed. "Okay."

"You can go." When the door shut again, the headmistress dropped back into her chair. "That child drives me crazy. She's bright and beautiful and completely impossible."

"I don't understand what happened," Nola said. She looked tired and stressed, which Mason knew could not be his fault since he'd been halfway across the country. "When we worked together last week, she seemed solid on all of the material the tests covered."

"I'll have Sharon work with her on the test anxiety, though I don't know if that will make up fifteen points on her grades. Mason, have you got any suggestions?"

He was tired and stressed, too. "To be honest, I think sometimes you have to realize you're going to lose, regardless of what you do. We can't save every one of these girls, Jayne. You and I both know it."

Nola was staring at him, eyes wide, jaw dropped in shock. "That's a terrible thing to say! What if you had given up on me twelve years ago? Where would I be?"

"I didn't have to give up on you, because you were willing to fight for yourself. Zara's not fighting. And none of us can force her to do so."

She turned to Jayne. "We have to keep trying. Zara is worth saving."

Jayne pressed her fingers against the bridge of her nose. "I agree. But Mason has a point—we can't do this for her. Zara must want to succeed."

Leaving Tommy's office a few minutes later, Nola didn't

wait for him to catch up with her but stalked straight across the hall, past workmen sanding red paint out of the marble, through the double doors and into her classroom.

Mason arrived a minute later. "At least we didn't have to play volleyball today."

"Small comfort," she growled as she threw books from her desk into her briefcase.

Between Nola's anger and Zara's resentment, the afternoon's tutoring session was a spectacular failure. Mason finally gave in to his own temper and stomped outside to help Garrett with the animals. When he returned half an hour later, they'd left the house.

"Women," he muttered, straightening the papers they'd left scattered across his table. He glanced at the telephone, wondering when—if—a call from the boys' schools he'd interviewed with might come.

"A life without estrogen," he promised himself. "What could be simpler?"

THOUGH THE OTHER teachers, including Mason, had told her what to expect, Nola was surprised by the rising level of tension she sensed in her students as the week passed. Even girls who had offered no trouble in the past began passing notes in class and whispering during her lectures, while failing to turn in their homework. Girls who had given her problems became nearly impossible to control.

And all because of the spring dance.

Classes ended at noon Friday, acknowledging the fact that not a single student would be paying attention that afternoon. Buses were scheduled to take girls into town on Saturday to have their hair and nails done and to make any last-minute purchases. Mealtimes buzzed with intense conversation as girls participated in the ages-old female ritual of deciding what to wear.

Nola stood at the center of this earthquake—the dining hall being transformed back into a ballroom. Tables and chairs had been removed and the protective mats covering the wood floor taken up. A few dozen bales of straw had arrived, compliments of Ruth Ann. Bolts of midnight-blue cloth, stamped with silver stars, lay folded on the floor next to boxes filled with crepe-paper streamers and more silvery stars to hang from the ceiling.

No one seemed to know what to do with any of it.

Mason stood with his hands in his pockets, looking confused. "Where does all this stuff go?"

Nola stared at him in exasperation. "You came to the meetings. You heard the plans."

"That doesn't mean I understood them. I'm a guy—I'll do whatever needs to be done. But the creative part?" He flattened one hand an inch above his hair. "Right over my head."

Cindi Bateman picked up a trailing length of blue cloth. "What did we say this was for?"

"We wrap those bales over there with it," Kim Huff, a student on Mason's committee, explained. "Something like that."

Michelle Danvers popped her gum. "I thought we put the stars on the bales."

Nola blew out a long breath. "Mason, could you find us a tall ladder? Now, girls, let me show you what we talked about. Bring me five—no, wait, seven bales."

She listened patiently to the complaints about getting stuck by straw, having straw in one's clothes and straw in one's hair. "Now, help me get these arranged. Then we take some blue cloth, like this…"

For the next three hours, Nola directed the students and Mason as they transformed the room into a romantic country getaway. Despite his protests, Mason contributed several creative ideas, including lighting behind the bales to create a gentle glow.

At six, they all gathered at the back of the room and Mason flipped the light switches.

"Oooooh!"

"Cool!"

"Awesome!"

Nola glanced at Mason, who was grinning. "Looks great," he said. "The nicest decorations I can remember."

Indeed, the ballroom did resemble a country night under the stars, with the chandeliers flickering and stars glittering near the ceiling. Tomorrow evening, with darkness beyond the windows, Nola thought all the students would be pleased.

Then Michelle turned to her with a frantic expression. "What if the terrorist comes back? He could ruin everything!"

"That won't happen." Nola and Mason together closed the big double doors, and Nola turned the bolt to lock them. "See? Nobody's coming in from that direction. The windows are latched from the inside only. And Mrs. Werner locks up the kitchen tight at night. There's no other way in. So don't worry."

She sent the girls out through the kitchen to a picnic supper being served on the lawn. With a last check on the locked door, she and Mason followed.

At the kitchen counters, Mrs. Werner, her daughter and granddaughter were hard at work on refreshments for the dance. The granddaughter was a pretty girl about sixteen, with strawberry-blond hair and freckles. She glanced up from her work as Nola passed and gave a shy smile.

"Thank you for all the extra effort," Nola told them. "I think the dance will be a real success."

"Our pleasure," Mrs. Werner replied. "Carey, honey, cut those slices a little thinner."

"Yes, ma'am." The girl sighed, and squinted as she focused on her task again.

"Are you eating at the picnic?" Mason asked Nola, once they were outside.

Nola shook her head. "I'm in need of peace and quiet, plus a soft chair and a cup of hot tea."

"Sounds good." After a second, he added, "Wish I could join you."

"That would be nice." All week she'd been chafed by the fact that they couldn't share ordinary experiences, or even a private conversation. Their morning hours were precious, but short. "But we'd better not."

"No. I guess not." Mason cleared his throat. "So, anyway, I'll check on the decorations during the day tomorrow. Sam Malcolm said he'd station a security guard in the hall tonight. Since they've posted security at the gate to sign in visitors I doubt we'll have any problems. But why take a chance?"

"Exactly."

Another couple might have kissed goodbye, or hugged, or just squeezed each other's hands. Mason lifted an arm, as if he might touch her, then let it drop to his side. "See you tomorrow."

Nola couldn't stand to let him go so bleakly. "Early?"

For a second, the glint returned to his eyes. "Early."

RUTH ANN HAD ASKED if she could come to Pink's Cottage to dress for the dance. "It's more fun when you have someone to help you with your hair and makeup and stuff."

Nola had never experienced that kind of shared preparation. Even as a teenager at Hawkridge, she'd kept pretty much to herself. But she liked Ruth Ann. They had, to Nola's surprise, become friends. And so she would give it a try.

Her friend arrived at five o'clock on Saturday with a clothes bag and a satchel of shoes, lingerie and makeup.

"I'd appreciate any advice," she said, hanging her dress bag on the back of the bedroom door. "You're always so perfectly put together. I, on the other hand, am better at grooming horses than myself." She frowned at her reflection in the mirror. "Just once, I'd like to look really nice. Sam Malcolm will be there, you know."

Nola had scarcely noticed the security chief for the school, but now she pictured him, a strong-looking man with dark red hair and fair skin. "Are you interested in Sam Malcolm?"

Ruth Ann had taken down her sun-streaked ponytail. "In that he's an adult male and I'm twenty-nine and single, yeah, I'm interested." She tried to shape a French twist, then let her hair fall. "But I don't know him very well."

Nola smiled. "Maybe we can change that tonight."

When they left the house at seven, Ruth Ann, the Equestrienne, had been replaced by Ruth Ann the Socialite. She wore a simple black dress that left her shoulders bare and showed off her slim, strong legs. Her hair was secured in a flattering French twist, and several strands of Nola's pearls skimmed her throat and right wrist. Careful makeup accentuated her long lashes and the natural bloom in her cheeks.

"You look terrific," Mason said as he caught up with them.

"I agree." Ruth Ann laughed. "Nola works wonders."

"Yes, she does." His smiling gaze moved over Nola from head to toe. "I'm speechless."

Nola wore her favorite dress, an elegant sheath in graphite-gray silk, which shimmered when she moved and emphasized her curves. Diamond studs in her ears and a simple diamond bracelet on her wrist finished the look. Mason's beguiled expression was the only compliment she needed.

"You look good, yourself," Ruth Ann told him. "Dark suit, blue tie, white shirt. Very nice." She took his arm, and then he held out his other to Nola. "Maybe I'll save you a dance."

He bowed in her direction. "I'd be honored."

The dance started at eight o'clock, but Nola needed to arrive ahead of time to let the disc jockey into the ballroom.

He'd set up his equipment earlier in the day, so all that was left was to turn on the lights and get the music started.

"The security guard has a key," Mason said as they approached the Manor. "We can enter through the doorway from the hall." The graffiti on the outside of the building had been ruthlessly scrubbed away, and the faint marks remaining could no longer be deciphered. Gas lamps on either side of the front door blazed with light and electric candles glowed in the classroom windows on both the first and second floors, lending a romantic aura to the façade of the house. Large gardenia bushes from the Hawkridge greenhouse lined the front steps, filling the walk to the door with sweet, heady fragrance. Nola wondered if they were the same bushes used at the last dance she'd attended, twelve years ago.

In the entry hall, all traces of paint had been scoured away. Vases of roses and tulips sat on the various tables, with more gardenias placed on the staircase steps, to serve both decorative and crowd-control functions. All the girls knew that no one was permitted on the second floor of the building.

A security guard stood in front of the doors to the ballroom. "Haven't seen a soul all day, except the florist," he reported in response to Mason's question.

"The deejay should be here any minute," Nola said.

Mason nodded. "Then let's open up and get this show on the road."

The guard turned around, released the big brass lock and pulled back one side of the door as Mason opened the other. Nola and Ruth Ann stepped over the threshold. They stopped abruptly, and Nola pressed her fingers to her lips.

"Oh my God," she whispered. "It's ruined."

Chapter Fourteen

Standing just behind Nola, Mason couldn't believe his eyes. The bales of straw had been broken apart and scattered all over the room. Shreds of blue fabric littered the floor. Most of the silver stars he'd spent hours hanging from the ceiling had been pulled down.

Worse, the antique French chandeliers had been vandalized, their crystal teardrops shattered on the floor. Chocolates and cookies were spilled everywhere. Only the sound equipment had escaped unscathed.

He and Nola and Ruth Ann were still standing frozen with shock when Jayne Thomas arrived. She uttered a single word—loud, explicit and rude—then pivoted back to the entry hall.

"Sam Malcolm is calling the police," she said over her shoulder. "What we have to do now is salvage the dance. Buses from the military academy will be here in less than ten minutes. We'll get some of the boys to help us move the music equipment out to the terrace." Waving her arms, she stalked around the vast ruined space. "Take all these gardenias, the vases of flowers and the candles, too. Nola, tell Mrs. Werner we'll need some kind of replacement food, even if it's packaged cookies and soft drinks. Mason, you and Sam can deal with the police. This investigation must become top priority. God only knows what might happen at graduation otherwise."

By the end of the evening, they all agreed that it had been one of the nicest spring dances anyone could remember. The May night was warm, the sky like a black velvet tent dusted with diamond stars. The deejay turned out to be terrific, mixing new music with older, slower songs to keep the guests from getting bored. And somehow Mrs. Werner produced more chocolates, more cookies, sandwiches, chips and punch.

"How does she do it?" Ruth Ann asked as she lingered with Nola near a refreshment table. "Must be magic." She looked at the half-eaten cookie in her hand. "I know these snicker-doodles are magically adding inches to my thighs every time I take a bite."

A smile was the most Nola could manage. "You're too hard on yourself." She'd kept busy by searching the crowd for the girls in her classes, wanting to see their dresses and the boys they chose to dance with. She found Zara, wearing a gorgeous red dress, with her hair cascading onto her shoulders, dancing with one of the best-looking cadets. Or doing something similar to dancing, anyway. Their bodies melted together, barely moving from side to side, and their faces were scarcely a millimeter apart.

Just as she was wondering, for the thousandth time, if Mason would ever get free of the police, she saw him approaching along the terrace wall.

"They're more or less finished," he said, stopping beside Ruth Ann. "Quite a temper at work in that ballroom. Whoever it is, they're furious."

"But no clues?" Ruth Ann asked.

"No. It's like a locked-room mystery. The only way out was through the kitchen, but Mrs. Werner was there all day and she saw no one." He chuckled. "She didn't appreciate being questioned while she was trying to replace the refreshments. I've never seen her so mad."

They watched the students dance for another few minutes in silence. "I find it hard to believe I ever moved like that," Mason said. "And even harder to picture my own child twisting himself around some girl like a predatory boa constrictor." He turned to Ruth Ann. "We could give it a try."

She rolled her eyes. "I'll wait for a slow number, thanks all the same. Right now, I'm off to interrupt an 'inappropriate display of public affection.' And avoid eating more cookies."

As she left, Mason stepped closer to Nola, angling his body so he could watch the dance and see her face. "Are you okay?"

She released a deep breath. "Better now."

He smiled slightly. "Me, too."

They both faced the dance floor again. Nola stopped wringing her hands and let them rest at her sides. "Does anyone know how to stop this crazy person?"

"The police are planning a search of the entire campus tomorrow—dorm rooms, classrooms and the surrounding forest." He nodded at her expression of surprise. "Oh, yes. The girls will be outraged, and their parents as well, I'm sure. But I agree with them. There's no alternative."

The pounding beat of the music faded, to be replaced with a slow, jazzy melody. "Something to groove by," the disc jockey crooned into the microphone before turning up the volume.

"This one's made for dancing." Mason looked at her and lifted an eyebrow. "Do we dare?"

In the space of a moment, Nola fought a war between reason and desire. Holding his gaze, she said, "No."

He sighed. "I didn't think so." After another minute, he reached for a glass of punch from the table behind them. "I think I'll walk around for a while. See you later?"

"Of course." She couldn't blame him. Just standing there together, while the saxophone moaned, was torture.

Nola watched the students, and thought about her own last spring dance at Hawkridge. She'd connected with one the boys from the academy, a beanpole of a kid with problem skin and clammy hands. During the slow songs, she'd moved into his shaky embrace, closed her eyes and pretended he was Mason Reed.

She'd done the same, she realized, with all the other men in her life. None of them had equaled, let alone surpassed, her dreams of Mason. And though the reality was more complicated, less perfect than her fantasies, he was the only one she wanted. She loved him.

But she wasn't at all sure they could build a future together.

GARRETT CAME into the kitchen near noon on Sunday, just as Mason hung up the phone. "Is it lunchtime yet? Who were you talking to?"

Mason glanced at the clock. "Sure, we can get something to eat. Grandmother left us a mountain of food in the fridge." With the last of his interviews finished, the Chances had left that morning to go home. The parting had been polite, but not warm.

"Did she leave roast beef? Can we have sandwiches?"

"You got it." He bent into the refrigerator, pulling out the necessary ingredients and piling them on the counter.

"Who was on the phone?" Garrett asked again.

Time to quit stalling. "That was the headmaster of a school in Arizona where I went for an interview. He…" Mason breathed deep. "He offered me a job."

Garrett dropped into a chair. "What kind of school?"

"A boys' school, grades six through twelve. You could go there and end up having me as your teacher in high school." He tried out a grin. "Weird, huh?"

Garrett didn't return the smile. "Are you gonna take it?"

"I don't know. I'd like to see if anyone else calls." Above all, he had to talk to Nola about the situation. He couldn't make a decision without her input. "What do you think about Arizona?"

"It's hot."

Mason spread mustard on a slice of bread. "This place is in the northern part of the state, so it's not so much of a desert. You could spend weekends at the Grand Canyon. You'd love that, I bet. Rafting the river, camping, hiking—"

"How would we move Rattles?"

Trust Garrett to get right to the sticking point. "I don't know. Maybe we'd need to find somebody here to take care of him for us, so he could stay in his natural home."

"Leave him behind?" From the tone of his son's voice, Mason might as well have suggested roasted raccoon for dinner.

He put down the knife and turned to look at the white-faced boy at the table. "Look, Garrett, don't get upset about any of this. Nothing's been decided. When the time comes, *if* the time comes, we'll figure out what's best for us and all the animals."

Garrett simply stared at him. After a long moment, he said, "I won't go."

Mason pretended he hadn't heard, and brought their lunch to the table. "Here you are. I'll get you a glass of milk."

As he reached the refrigerator, Garrett said, loudly, "I won't go!"

Milk carton in hand, Mason straightened up. "Where would you live?" he asked, keeping his tone even. He rested the milk carton on the rim of the glass to keep it from shaking.

"I'll take my animals and live with Grandma and Granddad. You go wherever you want."

Mason replaced the milk and brought the glass to the table. "I suppose that's an option. Your animals mean more to you than I do?" He sat down, took a bite of his sandwich, and nearly choked getting it down.

"No…" Garrett sat without touching his food. Tears dripped down his face. "Don't make me leave, Daddy. Please don't make me leave."

"Son—" Mason stood up, started around the table. But

Garrett escaped, knocking over his chair in his haste to leave the room. His footsteps pounded on the stairs, then his bedroom door slammed. The telltale squeak of bedsprings told the rest.

Mason set the chair upright then straddled it, propped his arms on the back and rested his head on them.

The good news—he had a new job, if he wanted one. The bad news—all he had to do, in this effort he was making to rebuild his own life, was ruin his son's.

And then he realized… Nola. Boston. Would Garrett refuse to go there, too? Would he have to choose between his son's happiness and the woman he loved?

The ringing of the telephone rescued him from an impossible dilemma. Dreading another job offer, he almost let the machine pick up, but at the last minute he grabbed the receiver.

"Mason, the police have found something," the headmistress said. "Can you be here at two o'clock?"

"Of course," he said automatically.

Hanging up, though, he could only wonder what kind of disaster had descended on Hawkridge now.

STANDING IN Jayne Thomas's office two hours later, Mason didn't know what to make of the items displayed on her desk. "Cartons of cigarettes. The paint cans—those I understand, and the latex gloves. But bags of candy and doughnuts? Tabloid newspapers and magazines? You found this in the woods behind the lodge?"

The Ridgeville police chief nodded. "Not all in exactly the same place. The junk food and magazines and smokes were in a small cave near the creek. We found the paint cans, the gloves and other stuff scattered between this building and there. I'd say the culprit ditched them while running away maybe to the stash or to the road. It's an easy walk from the cave to the highway."

"So someone's been coming in," Nola said, "for quite a long time, building up a collection of goodies, and then escalating into vandalism. But why?"

"Or else," Sam Malcolm said in his slow voice, "one of the girls has been going out."

Mason didn't like to think about the name that had popped into his mind. He glanced at Nola, and knew she'd had the same thought.

"I find that almost impossible to believe," Tommy said from across the room. "Our girls have their troubles, but I don't know of a single one who would take out her anger on the school itself." She looked at Mason and then Nola. "Do either of you…?"

He didn't answer fast enough, and Tommy's eyes widened in shock. "You think Zara Kauffman could have done this?"

"No," Nola said quickly, although the police chief was already writing down the name. "No, I don't think so."

Mason heard a trace of doubt in her tone. "You're not sure?"

"Of course I'm sure. Zara wouldn't do this. She's a rule-breaker, but—"

"Have you ever had a suspicion that this girl might be leaving campus?" The chief stared at Nola. "Seen her somewhere you didn't expect her to be?"

Nola's hesitation answered the question. "I've never actually seen her off campus. I suggested the possibility once when we were talking, and she didn't deny it."

He took more notes. "We'll need to talk to Zara Kauffman. Is she available?"

"I'm sure she is." Tommy placed a call to the dormitory. "I sincerely doubt she had anything to do with the vandalism. How could she go to the dance last night and act as if nothing had happened if she'd been the one to destroy the decorations?"

In the silence that followed, the phone rang. Tommy's brows drew together as she listened. "I'll be right up." She put the handset down and got to her feet. "Zara's door is locked, and she's not answering. I'm going up there."

"I'll send a couple of men with you," the chief said, following her out.

Nola stared at Mason, her hands gripped together at her waist. "You don't think Zara would...would hurt herself?"

"No, I don't. I think we're running off half-cocked in the wrong direction." He looked over at Sam Malcolm. "I'm going to walk Nola home. You can reach me at my place."

Sam nodded. "No problem."

The day was misty and cool, with showers dampening all but the strongest urge for outdoor activity. A few girls could be seen running and a couple were out on the volleyball court, but after last night's excitement, most students were sleeping or catching up with their homework.

"She didn't do this." Nola pounded one fist into the other palm. "I'm sure of it."

Mason walked with his hands gripped together behind his back—the only way he could keep from reaching for her. "I hope she's got some kind of proof. Because I'm going to have to go back in there at some point and tell them what Garrett told me."

"What did he say?"

"He let slip that he saw Zara at the pizza parlor the night you and I had dinner in town. She was there with one of the boys from the military academy—Garrett could tell by the haircut."

"Oh." Her tone conveyed the doubts that information raised. "Right."

They walked to her garden gate. As always, Nola went inside and closed the gate between them. "I would ask you in for tea, but..."

He shook his head. "That's okay. I should get home and let Ruth Ann go back to her horses. Garrett was sulking in his room when I needed to leave, so I asked her to stay with him."

Smiling, Nola asked, "What's upset him today? Did you make him do his homework before the absolute last minute?"

He'd hoped to have this talk in private, but they never knew when they'd have the chance to be alone. "Nothing so easy. I've been applying for a new teaching position, interviewing at different schools around the country. Today, I got a call offering me a job. In Arizona." He shrugged and gave a half-hearted laugh. "Garrett doesn't think he'd like Arizona."

Her smile faded as he spoke. She gazed at him in silence for several moments, then stirred. "The trips you've been taking weren't conferences?"

Mason shook his head. "I'm sorry I didn't tell you before now. Call it male pride—I figured I'd keep quiet, so if nobody wanted to hire me I wouldn't have to admit it. But now I know I'm marketable, at least."

"Are you going to take the job?" Her usually smooth voice squeaked a little, like a rusty hinge.

"I don't know. It's not my first choice. In fact, I really need to talk to you about that." He glanced over his shoulder and saw a group of girls walking back from the riding stable. "But not here and not now. As soon as this situation with Zara gets resolved we can go to dinner, or maybe you can just come over. Exams are almost here—the girls won't be paying attention to us much longer." He took a risk, touching the back of her wrist with the tips of his fingers.

And was shocked when Nola took a long step back. "I don't think that's necessary."

"I'd say it is. You've got to know by now that I'm not imagining the rest of my life without you in it. I need to adjust my plans accordingly."

"I don't know any such thing."

"Nola?" Mason had a feeling he'd unwittingly stepped into a puddle of tar. "What are you saying?"

She folded her arms across her breasts and took another

step backward. "Consulting me on your plans has never been necessary."

"If you're talking about Gail…"

"I know our friendship always meant something different to me than it meant to you." Her indrawn breath was unsteady. "As far as you were concerned, I was just another student, a problem child like all the rest. You were in control—you had access to my file, to the notes from my sessions with therapists, to my personality tests. You could read about my doctors' visits."

"I never did that."

"Now, I've grown up. I'm an adult but you still have the upper hand. You ask your probing questions, and I answer like a good little girl. I've held nothing back." She made a slicing motion with her hand. *"Nothing!"*

Then she closed her fingers into a fist. "But you can't manage to share the most important fact of your life with me—that you're changing jobs. Leaving Hawkridge.

"What if I had dreams, Mason? What if I'd been thinking about sharing my life with you? Don't you think it would have mattered to know that I could, in fact, ask you to come to Boston with me? Can you imagine, for one moment, the torture it's been to think I might have to choose between the career I've built and living beside the man I love with all my heart? And all you had to do, to spare me this pain, was be honest."

Her hand dropped to her side, and she turned toward the cottage.

Mason reached out and grabbed her wrist. "Nola, I'm sorry. I didn't realize—but I should have. There's been a lot going on. And what's between us has happened fast. Let's back up, set things right. We belong together."

She shook her head. "You're right—there is a lot going on. Too much. And what's to say Garrett would want to move to Boston any more than he wants to move to Arizona?"

Mason opened his mouth, but she wouldn't let him speak.

"It's too complicated, Mason. I need a clear mind to pursue my research. I need peace and a simple life. I love you, but I can't be with you."

Though he called after her, she didn't turn back. The door to Pink's Cottage shut firmly with Nola inside.

Mason wouldn't have been surprised if the entire student body was standing there listening when he turned around. But the lawn and the walks were empty. None of the girls had witnessed his argument with Nola. Not a single soul, not even Ruth Ann, was privy to the way he'd completely screwed up the rest of his life.

Cold comfort, that was.

NOLA STOOD in her kitchen, shivering, with a mug of tea between her palms. Mason hadn't told her. Hadn't respected her enough to be frank.

...or to tell her the truth. Instead, he simply pretended she didn't exist. No more smiles across the classroom, no more waves in the hallway or out on campus. He didn't answer his phone at the office—the secretary always told her he would call back. But he didn't. He didn't answer the phone at home, either, didn't return her messages.

Worse, he'd stopped taking appointments for individual help sessions. He told all his classes that he'd established a new policy about never meeting with fewer than three girls at a time. Did he realize they would all know why?

Wasn't it enough that he didn't love her, that his rejection had broken her heart? Did he have to humiliate her in front of the entire school, too?

She thought about sending him the notes she'd received from other girls, the evil, spiteful, gloating messages waiting on the floor when she woke up in the morning or slipped under her door as she tried to study.

He wouldn't care. He didn't look at her once during the

spring dance, though she'd ordered a terrific yellow gown from New York and had spent hours at the beauty shop to look gorgeous just for him. He'd smiled and talked with most of the senior girls, but he hadn't come near her. All year long, she'd dreamed of dancing in his arms. Instead, she went back to her room and ripped the dress into shreds.

What the hell? She'd be leaving Hawkridge in a matter of days, shaking off the dust from this stupid school and never coming back. She could always give them money. But they'd never see her face again.

"Two weeks," Nola told herself after a sip of tea. "In two weeks, you'll be gone." Finals would end, the girls would graduate and then she'd return to Boston and never, ever set foot south of Washington, D.C., again.

First, however, she had Zara to look out for, since no one else would. Grabbing a sweater, she left the cottage and headed back to the Manor.

She knocked on the closed door of Jayne's office, but didn't wait to be invited inside. Four people turned to stare as she barged in—Jayne, Sam, the police chief—and Zara.

The headmistress got to her feet. "Nola, I'm afraid we're busy with Zara. I can call you—"

"I think I need to be here," Nola said. "Zara should have someone on her side."

The police chief snorted, and even Sam Malcolm looked annoyed.

Jayne gave her a reproving look. "There are no sides right now. We're just asking questions."

A noise in the outer office turned the five of them to face the door. This time, Mason stood on the threshold.

"It's getting crowded in there." He flashed a slight grin at Jayne, but didn't meet Nola's eyes.

"Yes, it is," the headmistress said sharply. "What do *you* want?"

He came into the office and moved to stand behind Zara's chair. "I got to thinking, on my way home, that Zara might need someone on her side."

The police chief growled. "There are no sides, yet!"

Mason shrugged. "Then you won't mind if I just listen, will you?"

"I have an even better idea," Nola said. She found herself the focus of three glares, plus Zara's habitual frown and Mason's interested gaze. "Why don't you give us a few minutes alone with Zara? We're her mentors—maybe she'll feel better about talking to us, and we can get to the bottom of this situation."

Chapter Fifteen

The door closed behind Jayne, Sam and the chief. Then Zara spun around, splitting her suspicious stare between Mason and Nola.

"If you think you're gonna bully me into a confession, give it up. I'm not confessing to something I didn't do."

"So tell us what you did do." Nola sat down in the chair beside Zara's. "The cigarettes and food are yours, right?"

"Yeah."

Mason came around and leaned his hips against Tommy's desk. "Why did you choose that place? Why not somewhere closer to the dorm?"

"'Cause I'd have to carry it across campus. People would see, and wonder where it came from."

Mason nodded. "And where *did* the stuff come from?"

Zara looked down at her hands in her lap. "Town."

"You went to town? Not walking, right?"

"A couple of times I caught a ride on the highway." She glared at Nola. "I know it's dangerous. Stupid."

Nola nodded. "I'm glad you were lucky. You found another ride, I take it?"

"Owen. A guy from Ridgefield Academy. He keeps a car in town."

"The boy Garrett saw you with at the pizza parlor? The one you danced with last night?"

She nodded. "He would pick me up and drop me off. I'd hide what I bought in the cave and bring it back to my room, a little at a time."

"A smart plan." Nola leaned back. "Do you think there's a chance Owen could be the vandal?"

"No way. He doesn't care about Hawkridge one way or the other. Wouldn't a person who does things like this have to be really furious?"

"That's my theory," Mason said. "Can you think of anybody like that?"

"Besides me?" The girl grinned at the startled expressions on both Nola's face and Mason's. "Just kidding." Staring down at her hands, watching one thumb circle the other, she seemed to be considering options.

She looked up suddenly. "Owen's girlfriend. She knows he's seeing somebody from Hawkridge. He canceled their regular Saturday date to be here last night."

"Do you know her name?" Mason asked.

"Carey," she said. "That's all I know. Just Carey."

Mason blew out a long breath, his eyes on Nola's. "That's enough."

ONLY JAYNE THOMAS was allowed to go with the police when they questioned Mrs. Werner's granddaughter, Carey Inman.

Jayne reported back to Mason and Nola on Monday afternoon. "She wasn't sure which one of the girls the cadet was seeing until last night, so her rage was directed at the entire school." She sighed and relaxed in her chair. "As soon as Mrs. Werner gave her a stern look, she broke down and confessed everything. Poor girl. I wish we could bring her here for help."

"Where will she go?" Nola asked.

"A juvenile facility in the eastern part of the state, for two years. Then she'll be on her own, I suppose."

"She has time to change," Mason said gently. "I hope she appreciates the opportunity."

"Meanwhile," Nola replied, "we have to ensure that Zara makes use of hers."

They worked with her every class day for the remaining two weeks, cooperating, even joking together, as friendly colleagues might. But Nola avoided all personal contact with Mason. She could tell he was doing the same, and she spent her sleepless nights calculating how many minutes of this torture she had left to survive before she could leave North Carolina for good.

Final examinations began on the Wednesday after Memorial Day. One week later, all the tests were finished and graded. With her two-timing cadet out of the picture, Zara scored high enough on her physics exam to bring her final grade up to a C. Her math final didn't go as well, but she earned a D in the course for the semester and a C for the year. She would graduate with her class. Kathy Burns, her art teacher, even persuaded her to rethink an application to art school.

By the Friday afternoon of graduation day, Nola had packed most of her luggage. She'd booked a Sunday-afternoon flight out of Asheville, which would put her back in Boston late that night. The other option was to leave at dawn, but she couldn't bring herself to drive away in the dark.

Ruth Ann stopped by to walk with her to the graduation ceremony itself. "The saddest part about Carey Inman," she said, "is that her grandmother has decided to retire. Lunch today was the last meal Mrs. Werner will ever prepare for Hawkridge."

"That is too bad. Maybe she'll write a cookbook. Then I could find somebody to make those rolls for me on a daily basis."

"Good idea." Ruth Ann stumbled over a crack in the path. "Damn it, why do we have to wear heels? Not to mention the torture of sitting on a hard chair for two hours in a dress. I wish they would let us wear slacks, or else robes I could put on over a pair of shorts."

Nola smiled at her friend. "You're a tomboy through and through, aren't you?"

"I'm afraid so. And I don't imagine there are too many men out there in their thirties who are interested in tomboys."

"Oh, I suspect you'll find one. He might not realize himself just what he wants until he meets you."

"Says Ms. Optimist, as she walks away from a great guy who would do anything in his power to make her happy. Did you see them over the Memorial Day weekend?"

"No."

"Are you planning to talk to Mason before you leave?"

Nola didn't reply.

"Don't think not answering will shut me up. This is just a lovers' quarrel, right? You're going to forgive him and live happily ever after, aren't you?"

"Has Mason talked to you?"

"Not a word. I'm just second-guessing."

"My advice to you, then, is to stay away from racetracks and casinos."

For once, Ruth Ann did not have a comeback.

At Hawkridge graduations, the faculty filed in quietly just before the ceremony began and sat in the first two rows of chairs on the ballroom floor, with parents and guests behind them. Then, with the audience and faculty standing, the graduates processed to the string quartet rendition of "Pomp and Circumstance" and took their seats on the dais, behind the honored guests and Jayne Thomas.

As they sat down and Jayne rose to welcome the guests and introduce their speaker, Nola realized she was sitting directly behind Mason. That had not been the situation at this morning's rehearsal, and she strongly suspected someone had manipulated the seating plan. She couldn't make a fuss, however, so she would simply have to keep her mind on the speaker.

But as Ridgeville's mayor offered the graduating students his many long-winded ideas about opportunities for women in the twenty-first century, Nola found keeping her thoughts away from Mason to be impossible. The mayor droned on in his singsong voice while the June breeze, coming through the open windows, played with the delicate curls clinging to Mason's shirt collar in much the same way she loved to do. His shoulders were strong and broad beneath his dark tan suit jacket. Even if he'd changed seats just to torment her, she couldn't be angry at having these last few minutes to enjoy being close to the man she loved.

Ruth Ann seemed to think it would be so simple. Forgive him, and all would be well. But forgiveness wasn't the issue— she understood why he'd chosen not to say anything about his job applications. A man should have some pride.

But a woman should, as well. And Nola had learned early that the surest way to keep her dignity intact was to avoid caring. She'd done a good job at protecting herself, overall, with one exception—Mason Reed.

Behind the podium, the mayor finished whatever he'd had to say, and everyone applauded. Mason shifted in his seat and his jacket stretched across his back, reminding Nola of the smooth skin underneath. His lime scent teased her nostrils. She recrossed her legs, folded her arms more tightly and focused on the salutatorian of the class, now giving her speech about being "open" to the world.

Yes, Nola thought, but that was also the way to get hurt. She'd opened herself to Mason twice, and both times found herself…well, abandoned, actually. Maybe that was just her ego talking, or her adolescent self. But she couldn't stake the rest of her life on a man who wouldn't make the same commitment.

The valedictorian spoke next, a lovely girl with shining brown hair who'd aced Nola's calculus class. She spoke to her classmates about following their dreams, using the foundation Hawkridge had given them.

Nola reflected that Hawkridge had given her dreams, too—the awareness of her talents and the chance to use them properly. Mason had played a big part in that process. And during this visit—this reunion—he'd fulfilled the one dream she'd never believed would come true. He'd become a part of her. Now she would have to learn, again, to live without him.

Finally, the important part of the evening had arrived. Jayne returned to the speaker's stand. "At this time, it is my pleasure to present diplomas to the members of the graduating class." The string quartet began to play Vivaldi's *Four Seasons*, starting, appropriately, with "Spring."

As each girl's name was announced, she walked across the stage to shake hands with Jayne and the chairman of the Hawkridge board of directors. A photographer on the floor captured the triumphant moment. Families tended to forget themselves, to cheer and applaud, whistle and shout. Each presentation of a diploma represented a major achievement.

The list of graduates was arranged alphabetically, of course. A, B...G, H, J...and, at last, K. Nola sat forward in anticipation, and saw Mason do the same. Jayne looked at her roll, then at the graduates behind her. "Zara Elise Kauffman."

Grinning from ear to ear, Zara came across the stage to shake hands with Jayne. Whether her family made noise or not, Nola didn't know, because she and Mason were both applauding loudly. The rest of the faculty joined them. Zara might not be the valedictorian or the most likely to succeed. But she definitely deserved the award for Most Improved.

Nola was still clapping when she saw Zara turn to Jayne and say something. Jayne gave a slight shake of her head, and

Zara shrugged. Then she sidestepped the headmistress and walked to the edge of the platform.

"I just wanted everybody to know," she said, her voice carrying well in the stunned silence, "that I owe this diploma to the efforts of some very special people. All the teachers at Hawkridge are terrific—they care, and they work as hard as they can to help each girl succeed.

"When I was being stupid and getting ready to throw this away—" she held up the diploma "—two teachers rescued me. I want Mr. Reed and Ms. Shannon to know that I appreciate everything they did. Not just the tutoring, but also all the times they lectured me and yelled at me to get my head on straight." She gave a wry smile and the audience chuckled. "They loved me. And that made the difference."

Nola eased back into her chair and tried to wipe the tears from her cheeks without being too obvious. Down the row, Ruth Ann leaned forward to catch her attention and gave her a big grin. Beside Nola, Alice Tolbert grabbed her hand and squeezed hard.

In front of her, Mason didn't move. She had closed herself off from him, so they couldn't share this moment of joy.

And in that, she had failed both him and herself.

THE RECEPTION for graduates and their families had taken place at lunchtime. Mason skipped it, in case Nola wanted to go. But he looked for Zara after the graduation ceremony, hoping for a chance to give her his personal congratulations.

He found her in the middle of a large group of people—large both in stature and in number. She looked like a girl, for once, in a bright red dress, with her curly hair flowing free around her shoulders.

She saw him as he approached. "Hey, Mr. Reed." Without warning, she threw her arms around his neck and hugged him tight. "Thanks," she whispered in his ear.

"You're welcome," he said quietly, patting her waist carefully, hoping to avoid the bare skin revealed by her strapless dress. "Is, uh, this your family?"

"Yeah." She introduced him to her father, who continued the process—his son the doctor, his son the football player, his sons the A-students, his wife. "We're glad you helped Zara graduate," Mr. Kauffman said. "Don't know what she'll do next, though."

"I suspect she has plans," Mason drawled. "And we'll be even prouder of her one day than we are right now."

Just as he finished, Zara looked beyond him, and then darted off. Mason didn't have to look to see where she'd gone. He simply waited, tightening up inside to get through the next few minutes.

She returned with Nola in tow. "This is the other savior. Ms. Shannon." The same introductions were made.

Nola shook hands with Mr. Kauffman, then turned to his wife. "You must be very proud. Zara is quite talented and very smart." She sent the girl a wry smile. "Though sometimes lacking in motivation."

They all stood silent for a moment. There wasn't much to say. "Will you be here tomorrow?" Zara asked, looking at Mason and Nola both. "To say goodbye?"

"I'll be here," Mason assured her at the same time as Nola said, "Of course." The only thing they could do, at that point, was turn and walk away together.

"She hugged me." Nola rubbed her hands up and down her bare arms as they took the path toward Pink's Cottage. "She hugged me."

Mason shoved his hands in his pockets. "Me, too."

She gave him a sideways glance. "We made a difference in the rest of her life."

"A good feeling, isn't it?"

"Oh, yes."

They paused at the fork in the path that led to the cottage

on the right, or on to the lodge. She looked around them at the mountain night, with stars close enough to touch. "I'm going to miss this. Very much."

"I would." He'd spent most of the graduation ceremony trying to prepare something to say, some convincing argument to win her back. Right now, he couldn't remember a word of it.

"I just wanted to say…" He loosened his tie, dragged his fingers through his hair. "I want to apologize."

She started to speak, but he held up a hand. "I've been thinking back—twelve years back. You scared me, Nola. I couldn't admit it, but you did. You were a genius, you were lovely, you were sexy as hell. What was I supposed to do with a woman like that? I wasn't mature enough to handle what you offered with kindness, or concern. I just ran away."

"Mason…"

"I'm sorry you were hurt by the careless boy I was. Gail helped me grow up." He chuckled. "Garrett, even more so. And yet I still made a mess of things. I'm sorry for that, too."

Mason waited, but Nola didn't say anything.

"So, anyway… Good night. I'm sure I'll see you tomorrow." He walked toward home without looking back, and tried not to listen for the closing of the Pink's Cottage door.

But he couldn't help it—just before he went into the trees, he glanced over his shoulder. Nola still stood at the fork in the path, watching him walk away. Was that a good omen? Could he sleep tonight, believing she would change her mind?

Or was she simply saying a final goodbye?

NOLA VENTURED OVER to the dorm around ten on Saturday morning. Mr. Kauffman and his sons had loaded Zara's bags and boxes into their elephantine SUV and stood beside the doors, ready to depart.

Zara, wearing a black tank top with her camouflage pants and boots, seemed reluctant to join them. "It's gonna be a long drive," she said quietly. "He'll spend the whole way home telling me what I should do with my life."

"Tune him out," Nola suggested. "You're good at that."

Zara grinned at her. "You noticed, huh?"

"A time or two."

Once again, Zara gave her a hug. "I have your e-mail address. Don't put me on your spam list."

"I wouldn't think of it." Nola returned the embrace, squeezing back tears.

"Good." Zara pulled back, blinking quickly, running her index fingers under her lower lashes. "Between you and Mr. Reed, I'm gonna have black streaks on my face all day."

"You've already seen him?"

"He and Garrett were here real early. They were heading out to a soccer game."

"Ah. Well, good luck, Zara. Do let me know what's going on."

"Sure." She started toward the SUV, then turned and came back to Nola. "You and Mason belong together. He's about as bad now as I've ever seen him, since his wife died. If you can figure out a way to make it work, you ought to."

"Zara!" Mr. Kauffman held his wrist up and pointed to his watch. "Let's go."

"Okay!" She gave Nola a wave, then ran back and climbed into the car. In seconds, the SUV was out of sight.

Nola said a few more farewells and drifted back to the cottage. By noon, most of the graduates would be gone, though many of the younger girls would stay over the summer, taking classes in art, music, drama and sports, as well as academic subjects. The teacher she'd replaced would be able to return to work when the fall term started. Nola's sojourn at Hawkridge had ended.

Walking away from the Manor, she bypassed Pink's Cottage and headed for the hunting lodge. Mason and Garrett usually got home by lunch. If they hadn't yet arrived, she would wait for them on the porch.

But she found Garrett playing with his three-legged dog in the front yard. He ran down the path to meet her. "Hey, Ms. Shannon, did you come for lunch? Dad said it would be ready in a few minutes."

The dog proceeded to run circles around Nola, barking in excitement. "Hi, Garrett. Good dog." She reached down to pet the little dog, trying to keep her hand steady. Trying to believe all the noise wasn't the prelude to a bite.

At the sound, the two younger dogs came racing around the corner of the house and headed straight for her. Nola braced herself with her free hand on one knee. If she could just stay on her feet...

"Ruff, Ready! Stay!" Mason had come out on the porch. At his command, the two brown dogs crouched about ten feet away, panting and wagging their tails.

"No, it's okay," Nola told him. "I'm ready."

Mason gazed at her for a long moment. Then he called, "Okay, Ruff. Okay, Ready."

The dogs surged forward. Nola got her face licked from all directions, and she felt a little dizzy with all the dogginess swirling like water around her legs. But she got some pats in, and the tickle of the rough tongues against her hand made her laugh.

"Hey, Garrett." Mason waved both his arms toward the back of the house. "Take them for a walk in the woods."

The boy propped his hands on his hips. "You said lunch would be ready in a few minutes."

"It will be." Mason waved him away. "Go for a walk first."

"I'm starving," Garrett muttered. "Gimp, let's go for a walk. Are you coming? Are you? Let's go." The terrier danced after him and with a final lick at Nola, Ruff and Ready followed.

As boy and dogs disappeared, Nola went toward the front porch. Angel, the retriever, sat on the top step, gently wagging her tail.

"Hi, Angel." Nola touched her nose, petted her ears. "You've got such dignity, compared to all those young dogs. You're a good girl, aren't you?" Angel sighed and lay down with her head on her front paws. Sitting beside her, Nola continued to stroke the soft gold fur.

Mason wasn't sure what to do with himself. Should he sit beside her? Should he walk down the steps and stand gazing up at her, or look down from where he was? The thump of his heart in his chest made thinking a challenge.

Nola solved the problem by standing up again. She leaned back against the post behind her. "How have you been?"

"Pretty terrible. You?"

"About the same."

He said the only thing he could think of, a repetition of last night. "I'm sorry. I didn't mean to hurt you."

"I know. I didn't mean to be hurt." She kept her eyes down, watching as she scratched in the dust on the step with one sandaled foot. "But why should I be any different than the rest of humanity?" Looking up, she caught his puzzled expression. "Everyone gets hurt, don't they? Gail's death was painful for you, for Garrett, for the Chances, though none of you deserved to be hurt. Gail certainly didn't intend to make you sad."

Mason nodded. "That's true."

"Most of the people in my life haven't meant to cause me pain. My parents, the guardians—"

Mason raised his eyebrow at that, and she said, "Okay, the guardians were thoughtless. But I took all these experiences—including what happened with you in high school—and used them as an excuse to retreat from relationships. As you said, I walled off my heart."

After clearing his throat, he asked, "Has that changed?"

She straightened up away from the post. "How could it not? Zara, and the other girls, Garrett and his animals, the teachers and you, most of all, have broken down the walls. The gate's unlocked and I wouldn't close it again if I could."

She stepped over Angel to stand in front of him. "I love you, Mason Reed. That fact will never change, whether we can make a life together or not. I'm hoping, though, that there's a way we can share ourselves, our joys and concerns, for a long, long time."

When he didn't say anything, she began to look anxious. "Have I made a mistake? Is this not what you want? Did I ruin my last chance?"

All he could do was shake his head—his throat had closed down completely. He took her hand, though, and led her into the house, into the parlor, and gestured for her to sit down.

She sat, watching him with worried eyes. "Mason? Are you all right?"

"Yes," he whispered. Then he cleared his throat and tried again. "I'm okay. Just…well, stunned." He went to the closet, pulled out the gift he'd hidden there and brought it back to the sofa.

He set it on her lap. "I thought I should replace this."

"Oh, Mason." She smiled, running her hand over the smooth leather of a Louis Vuitton lingerie bag exactly like the one she'd sacrificed for Homer. "You didn't have to."

"I know. I also bought you a small going-away gift. It's inside."

Nola felt all the blood drain from her head. A going-away gift. He expected her to leave. She swallowed hard. "Let me see what's in here." She unfastened the buckles and pulled apart the sides of the valise to peer inside.

On the very bottom sat a turtle—a small, elegant, red lacquer turtle with designs carved into its shell. "Mason, how beautiful." She brought it out. "Thank you so much." She had to leave now, before she fell apart.

"It's a box," Mason said. "You should open it."

Her fingers were shaking and he would see that, but what could she do? Clumsily she separated the shell, which formed the lid, from the rest of the turtle. "That's ni— Oh." Inside, resting on the red velvet lining, was an uncut diamond the size of a pecan shell.

"It's flawless," Mason said, his voice rough. "I wanted to let you make the decisions on how it's cut and set. I want you to be my partner in every decision of my life, large and small. I want you to be my wife. I swear, I'll be with you as long as there's a breath left in my body."

Nola held up a cautious finger, asking him to wait. Very carefully, she set the stone in the center of the box and replaced the lid. She set the turtle back inside the lingerie bag and buckled the straps.

Then she started crying and laughing and falling apart, just as she'd feared. "Oh, Mason, yes. Yes, of course!"

He sat down beside her and pulled her into his arms, while she threw herself at him and cinched her arms around his neck. Mason kissed her forehead and cheeks and chin and throat, then captured her mouth for a breathless, passionate eternity. Nola feasted on the pleasure of his hands, his lips, his body against hers. The prospect of knowing this joy for the rest of her life was almost too much to imagine.

"What are you doing?"

They broke apart to find Garrett standing in the doorway, staring at them.

"We're kissing," Mason said after a few seconds of shock. "Nola and I would like to get married. What do you think?"

Garret considered for a moment. "Cool," he said finally.

Nola held out her hand to him and drew him closer. "Garrett, would it be awful if you came to Boston to live? We haven't talked about it," she said with a glance at Mason. "But that's where my work is. Do you think you could be happy living somewhere besides Hawkridge?"

Mason found himself holding his breath and deliberately took in some air. Garrett, meanwhile, stared at the floor, rubbing the side of his nose with a dirty finger.

Then, still without saying anything, he looked up at the ceiling for a long moment.

"Garrett, son, I'm dying here."

He gazed at Nola. "Would Dad teach there, too?"

"I might," Mason answered. "Or—who knows—maybe I'll go back to school myself, pick up an engineering degree. Start designing planes for a living."

Nola gazed at him with tears streaming down her cheeks.

Grinning, Mason looked at his son. "So what do you think?"

"Cool," Garrett said again. But…" He looked at Mason with pleading in his eyes. "Could we please have lunch first? I'm starved!"

The next book in our
THE STATE OF PARENTHOOD miniseries
takes us west to the mountains of
Arizona and Bear Creek Ranch.
Cathy McDavid's COWBOY DAD
tells the story of a man who was born
to be a father—he just doesn't know it until
he meets Natalie Forrester and
her adorable baby, Shiloh.

Chapter One

Natalie Forrester stood on the sweeping front porch and watched the old truck rumble down the long road, its tires kicking up a funnel cloud of brown dust. The driver pulled a dilapidated horse trailer that rattled and banged as if it might fall apart with each pothole it hit.

As manager of guest services at Bear Creek Ranch, Natalie considered herself quite adept at determining a visitor's purpose based on the vehicle they drove. This fellow, in his seen-better-days pickup, was either a local from nearby Payson or a cowboy looking for work. Since she didn't recognize the vehicle, cowboy got her vote. Her hunch grew stronger when the driver continued through the ranch in the direction of the barn and corrals.

Whoever he was, he'd be disappointed when he met Natalie's father, head of the resort's guest amenities. Bear Creek Ranch was fully staffed for the upcoming season, scheduled to begin in a mere ten days.

And speaking of the upcoming season, Natalie had a lot of work ahead of her. Break time was over. Her feet, however, refused to heed her brain's command to turn around and march inside. The weather was unusually warm for February, the afternoon particularly balmy. According to the thermometer hanging by the front door of the main lodge, the temperature hovered in the mid-sixties. Quite nice, even for the southern edge of Arizona's rim country, which enjoyed considerably milder winters than its northern counterpart.

Natalie leaned her shoulder against a column built from a tree that had been harvested in the nearby woods about the time President John F. Kennedy took office. The wood, once rough and unfinished, had been worn smooth through the decades by thousands of shoulders belonging to the guests of Bear Creek Ranch.

She never tired of the view from the front porch. Majestic pines towered to where wispy clouds floated in a sky so blue no artist could truly capture the vibrant hue. Behind the trees, the nearby Mazatzal Mountains rose, their stair-step peaks covered in snow much of the year. Bear Creek, the ranch's namesake, could be easily reached by foot from any of the resort's thirty-three cabins. Clear and clean, the creek teemed with trout and was a favorite with guests wanting to drop a line and test their luck.

Natalie had been born on this ranch, in the same cabin her parents occupied today. Like her younger sister, Sabrina, she'd grown up on the ranch. Unlike Sabrina, Natalie stayed on after reaching adulthood, learning the hospitality business from the ground up.

She wasn't related to the Tuckers, the family who had owned the ranch since it was constructed back when the railroad still made a stop at the old Bear Creek Station. But she and her parents were treated like family in many ways, and her loyalty to the Tuckers ran deep.

The front screen door banged open, rousing Natalie from her woolgathering. Alice Gilbert, the ranch's office manager and Jake Tucker's personal assistant, popped her head out the door.

"I think Shiloh's awake." She wore the expression of a

person who had no experience with babies and wasn't interested in acquiring any.

"Thanks."

Pushing off the column, Natalie hurried inside. Her shoes clicked softly on the highly polished hardwood floors as she crossed the lobby toward the front desk. Alice had already disappeared into her small office, which was situated right next to Jake Tucker's larger one.

Natalie didn't have the luxury of a private office. Her position required she be available to guests whenever she was on duty and sometimes when she wasn't. Since she stood—or walked or ran if necessary—more often than she sat while working, the compact computer station tucked behind the reception desk suited her needs just fine.

It was the supply room next to her computer station that Natalie entered, listening intently. No crying. Maybe Alice had been wrong. Tiptoeing, Natalie made her way to the portable crib on the floor in the center of the supply room. A Mother Goose night-light provided just enough illumination for her to make out the tiny baby stirring in the crib.

Shiloh.

As always, Natalie's heart melted at the sight of her beautiful three-month-old daughter. How did she ever get so lucky? What had been a scary unplanned pregnancy turned into the greatest joy of her life.

"Hey there, sweetie pie." She bent and reached into the crib. Lifting Shiloh, she put the baby to her shoulder, kissing a crown of feather-soft hair as she did. "You hungry?"

In response, Shiloh wiggled and mewed and made sucking noises with her tiny mouth.

"Let's go, then."

Natalie left the storage room/nursery and headed toward Jake Tucker's office. Her boss had given her permission to use his office when he wasn't there, to nurse Shiloh in privacy.

Alice didn't much care for the arrangement, but she had no say in the matter. Jake insisted.

Sitting in the overstuffed leather chair behind Jake's desk, she swiveled to face the window. Shiloh was a good baby in most ways, a blessing considering her slightly unusual day-care circumstances. Natalie nursed the baby and contemplated the changes she'd need to make soon.

The Tuckers had been generous with her since Shiloh's birth. They'd given her six weeks' maternity leave with pay and then allowed her to use the storage room as a makeshift nursery after she returned to work. Natalie's mother, who'd retired from Natalie's job two years ago, watched the baby for a couple hours in the morning. Jake's oldest daughter helped out when she got home from school.

It was those hours in between that were the problem. Natalie couldn't keep Shiloh with her during the day when the ranch reopened for the new season. Hiring a part-time nanny made the most sense. Finding a trusted candidate she could afford on her modest budget wouldn't be easy.

Balancing Shiloh in her lap, Natalie rubbed the baby's back and waited for a burp. When Shiloh showed no interest in nursing more, Natalie buttoned her blouse. Not an easy task with a baby in her lap. She started when the door unexpectedly opened and hurried to smooth her disarrayed clothing. Shiloh gave a fussy cry in response.

"Just a second," Natalie said, feeling her cheeks flush. Despite having permission to be there, she was nonetheless embarrassed. She stood up and turned around, Shiloh cradled in her arms, an apology on the tip of her tongue.

Only it wasn't Jake Tucker who stood just inside the doorway. This man was a complete stranger. It took Natalie a moment to compose herself.

"May I help you?" Her voice squeaked slightly.

"Sorry to disturb you, ma'am." He removed his battered

cowboy hat. "The lady out front didn't tell me anyone was in here."

"Not your fault." Natalie mustered her best be-nice-to-the-guests smile. Alice's oversight may or may not have been intentional. No point getting upset about it.

"The fellow down at the stables told me to wait here for Tucker."

Two things about the man's statement struck Natalie as odd. First was the fact her father sent the cowboy to the main lodge. Even if they were looking to hire another hand, her father didn't need Jake's approval for that.

Second, no one Natalie knew or had ever met referred to Jacob Tucker by his last name alone. Family and close friends called him Jake. Everyone else, including Natalie except when they were in private, called him Mr. Tucker.

"Did Alice phone him for you?"

"If that's the lady out front, I believe she did. Said he'd be right along."

He smiled at Natalie then, and she was surprised to find herself thinking what an attractive man he was. Dark brown eyes and even darker hair hinted at a Hispanic heritage. His shoulders were wide but proportionate to his height and well muscled. This cowboy, in his faded jeans and worn-at-the-elbows work shirt, was accustomed to hard physical labor. It was a look he carried well.

"All right then." Natalie took a step toward the door, intending to leave. Her curiosity was definitely piqued, but this man's meeting with Jake was none of her business.

"Your baby's very pretty."

His words stopped her. She received many compliments on Shiloh, but rarely from men and never from men who were strangers.

"Thank you," she replied awkwardly.

His smile warmed, and Natalie relaxed. She worked with

people on a daily basis and met all types. Though appearances could be deceiving, she was a quick and fairly accurate judge of character. This cowboy didn't strike her as a troublemaker or a creep. If anything, she sensed the opposite in him. There was a sadness underlying his pleasant manner. Telltale, but definitely there.

"Her father must be very proud of her," he said.

"I wouldn't know." Her response came unexpectedly. She didn't reveal much to anyone about Shiloh's absent father, preferring to dodge questions rather than reply.

"His loss," the man said simply.

"Yes, it is," Natalie said just as simply, and automatically held a dozy Shiloh closer. "I'd best go."

He inclined his head. "Maybe I'll see you around the ranch."

There was nothing flirtatious about his statement, but Natalie still kept her tone professional. "If you're staying, that's likely."

"I'm staying."

"You sound very sure."

"It's taken me two years to get here. And now that I am, I'm not leaving. For any reason," he added.

*Ladies, start your engines with a sneak preview
of Harlequin's officially licensed
NASCAR® romance series.*

Life in a famous racing family comes at a price

All his life Larry Grosso has lived in the shadow of his
well-known racing family—but it's now time for him to
take what he wants. And on top of that list is Crystal
Hayes—breathtaking, sweet…and twenty-two years
younger. But their age difference is creating animosity
within their families, and suddenly their romance is the
talk of the entire NASCAR circuit!

*Turn the page for a sneak preview of
OVERHEATED
by Barbara Dunlop.
On sale July 29 wherever books are sold.*

Rufus, as Crystal Hayes had decided to call the black Lab, slept soundly on the soft seat even as she maneuvered the Softco truck in front of the Dean Grosso garage. Engines fired through the open bay doors, compressors clacked and impact tools whined as the teams tweaked their race cars in preparation for qualifying at the third race in Charlotte.

As always when she visited the garage area, Crystal experienced a vicarious thrill, watching the technicians' meticulous, last-minute preparations. As the daughter of a machinist, she understood the difference a fraction of a degree or a thousandth of an inch could make in the performance of a race car.

She muscled the driver's door shut behind her and waved hello to a couple of familiar crew members in their white-and-pale-blue jumpsuits. Then she rounded the back of the truck and rolled up the door. Inside, five boxes were marked Cargill Motors.

One of them was big and heavy, and it had slid forward a few feet, probably when she'd braked to make the narrow parking lot entrance. So she pushed up the sleeves of her canary-yellow T-shirt, then stretched forward to reach the box. A couple of catcalls came her way as her faded blue jeans tightened across her rear end. But she knew they were good-natured, and she simply ignored them.

She dragged the box toward her over the gritty metal floor.

"Let me give you a hand with that," a deep, melodious voice rumbled in her ear.

"I can manage," she responded crisply, not wanting to engage with any of the catcallers.

Here in the garage, the last thing she needed was one of the guys treating her as if she was something other than, well, one of the guys.

She'd learned long ago there was something about her that made men toss out pickup lines like parade candy. And she'd been around race crews long enough to know she needed to behave like a buddy, not a potential date.

She piled the smaller boxes on top of the large one.

"It looks heavy," said the voice.

"I'm tough," she assured him as she scooped the pile into her arms.

He didn't move away, so she turned her head to subject him to a *back off* stare. But she found herself staring into a compelling pair of green...no, brown...no, hazel eyes. She did a double take as they seemed to twinkle, multicolored, under the garage lights.

The man insistently held out his hands for the boxes. There was a dignity in his tone and little crinkles around his eyes that hinted at wisdom. There wasn't a single sign of flirtation in his expression, but Crystal was still cautious.

"You know I'm being paid to move this, right?" she asked him.

"That doesn't mean I can't be a gentleman."

Somebody whistled from a workbench. "Go, Professor Larry."

The man named Larry tossed a "Back off" over his shoulder. Then he turned to Crystal. "Sorry about that."

"Are you for real?" she asked, growing uncomfortable with the attention they were drawing. The last thing she needed was some latter-day Sir Galahad defending her honor at the track.

He quirked a dark eyebrow in a question.

"I mean," she elaborated, "you don't need to worry. I've been fending off the wolves since I was seventeen."

"Doesn't make it right," he countered, attempting to lift the boxes from her hands.

She jerked back. "You're not making it any easier."

He frowned.

"You carry this box, and they start thinking of me as a girl."

Professor Larry dipped his gaze to take in the curves of her figure. "Hate to tell you this," he said, a little twinkle coming into those multifaceted eyes.

Something about his look made her shiver inside. It was a ridiculous reaction. Guys had given her the once-over a million times. She'd learned long ago to ignore it.

"Odds are," Larry continued, a teasing drawl in his tone, "they already have."

She turned pointedly away, boxes in hand as she marched across the floor. She could feel him watching her from behind.

* * * * *

Crystal Hayes could do without her looks,
men obsessed with her looks, and guys who think
they're God's gift to the ladies.
Would Larry be the one guy who could blow all
of Crystal's preconceptions away?
Look for OVERHEATED
by Barbara Dunlop.
On sale July 29, 2008.

REQUEST YOUR FREE BOOKS!
2 FREE NOVELS PLUS 2
FREE GIFTS!

American ★ Romance®

Heart, Home & Happiness!

YES! Please send me 2 FREE Harlequin American Romance® novels and my 2 FREE gifts (gifts are worth about $10). After receiving them, if I don't wish to receive any more books, I can return the shipping statement marked "cancel." If I don't cancel, I will receive 4 brand-new novels every month and be billed just $4.24 per book in the U.S. or $4.99 per book in Canada, plus 25¢ shipping and handling per book and applicable taxes, if any*. That's a savings of close to 15% off the cover price! I understand that accepting the 2 free books and gifts places me under no obligation to buy anything. I can always return a shipment and cancel at any time. Even if I never buy another book from Harlequin, the two free books and gifts are mine to keep forever.

154 HDN EEZK   354 HDN EEZV

Name	(PLEASE PRINT)	

Address		Apt. #

City	State/Prov.	Zip/Postal Code

Signature (if under 18, a parent or guardian must sign)

Mail to the **Harlequin Reader Service:**
IN U.S.A.: P.O. Box 1867, Buffalo, NY 14240-1867
IN CANADA: P.O. Box 609, Fort Erie, Ontario L2A 5X3

Not valid to current subscribers of Harlequin American Romance books.

Want to try two free books from another line?
Call 1-800-873-8635 or visit www.morefreebooks.com.

* Terms and prices subject to change without notice. N.Y. residents add applicable sales tax. Canadian residents will be charged applicable provincial taxes and GST. Offer not valid in Quebec. This offer is limited to one order per household. All orders subject to approval. Credit or debit balances in a customer's account(s) may be offset by any other outstanding balance owed by or to the customer. Please allow 4 to 6 weeks for delivery. Offer available while quantities last.

Your Privacy: Harlequin is committed to protecting your privacy. Our Privacy Policy is available online at www.eHarlequin.com or upon request from the Reader Service. From time to time we make our lists of customers available to reputable third parties who may have a product or service of interest to you. If you would prefer we not share your name and address, please check here. ☐

HAR08R

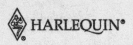

HARLEQUIN®

American ★ Romance®

CATHY McDAVID
Cowboy Dad

THE STATE OF PARENTHOOD

Natalie Forrester's job at Bear Creek Ranch
is to make everyone welcome, which is an
easy task when it comes to Aaron Reyes—the
unwelcome cowboy and part-owner. His
tenderness toward Natalie's infant daughter
melts the single mother's heart. What's not
so easy to accept is that falling for him means
giving up her job, her family and the only
home she's ever known....

***Available August
wherever books are sold.***

LOVE, HOME & HAPPINESS

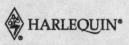

COMING NEXT MONTH

#1221 COWBOY DAD by Cathy McDavid

The State of Parenthood

Natalie Forrester's job at Bear Creek Ranch is to make everyone welcome. That's an easy task when it comes to Aaron Reyes, a cowboy whose tender treatment of Natalie's infant daughter melts the single mother's heart. Falling for him would be easy—if it didn't mean giving up her job, her family and the only home she's ever known....

#1222 FOREVER HIS BRIDE by Lisa Childs

The Wedding Party

Brenna Kelly just took that fateful walk down the aisle...as maid of honor at her best friend's wedding. But when the bride's a no-show, Brenna suddenly has to cope with a runaway wedding...and her own runaway feelings for the jilted groom—handsome Dr. Josh Towers.

#1223 BABY IN WAITING by Jacqueline Diamond

Harmony Circle

When Oliver Armstrong took in Brooke Bernard as his temporary roommate, he should have known the free-spirited beauty would promptly turn his life upside down. Especially when she found out she was pregnant. Now she wants Oliver to help her round up a suitable husband. But the ideal mate is closer than she realizes—right under the same roof!

#1224 A COAL MINER'S WIFE by Marin Thomas

Hearts of Appalachia

Single, with twin boys to raise, high-school dropout Annie McKee is torn between choosing hand-me-downs and charity from her Appalachian clan or leaving Heather's Hollow and finding a better future for her boys. But the proud widow might have another option—*if* she can accept handsome neighbor Patrick Kirkpatrick's avowal that there's nothing secondhand about love!

HARCNM0708